I've painted the Great Fish on my mural. I've painted its slaughter. I've painted many things. Something keeps dripping on my head from above, but I'm too focused to care now; I wipe it away and continue. I dream, then awaken and I paint, and then, when my eyes close from utter exhaustion, I dream again from the cold concrete floor before it is time to rise again. Sometimes, I think the only thing that wakes me is my own scream, dragging myself up, the brush still in my hand. Nightmares can mess you up permanently. Some people never come back from that shit. Whose voice? I'm no longer sure. I no longer care. There is one dream, persistent, a nightmare, which I am still unable to remember upon waking. It is the most horrible dream, a constant roaring in my ears, it is... I remember my mom, after she'd read to me and I'd closed my eyes and she thought I was asleep, lightly stroking my hair, saying what she wanted to say and knew would embarrass me during the daytime, but that I secretly adored, "Beautiful boy...my beautiful boy...shhh...my beautiful boy..." But the nightmare interferes, haunts all seventeen layers of my soul...

Once again to Amber

WITHIN

by Keith Deininger

Is this a dream?

I've known, I think, instinctively from the very beginning, he is dangerous.

Sometimes, he looks at me funny, appraising, smiling. He lets me work in my own way, at my own pace, and that's all I can ask for. He visits me sometimes when I'm working to ask a few simple questions, always circling back to how much time it will take me to finish. I can never tell him. I don't exactly know what I'm doing, what I'm creating—I only know that it has to be just right, that each brushstroke has to be precise, my subject shaped to perfection. There are entire days when I am forced to paint over what I have done because it isn't good enough. I only know that I am working toward something important, something meaningful and powerful. I have to trust in my artistic instincts. He tells me not to worry, that I'm doing a good job, but sometimes I wonder. He tells me not to think too hard about it, that true artistic expression comes from something deep within, yet larger than ourselves.

"Colin," Mr. Klimt says, looking me in the eyes. "It is not ours to question, but to create..."

PART ONE: THE PARTY

"There was much of the beautiful, much of the wanton, much of the bizarre, something of the terrible, and not a little of that which might have excited disgust."

—Edgar Allan Poe, *The Masque of the Red Death*

CHAPTER 1

KLIMT

People talked, of course. People said he'd once had a family, a loving wife, but she'd killed herself and their two daughters. People said his life was filled with tragedy, that he'd been bankrupt and destitute, despite his Harvard education, but that he'd made a triumphant return, come into a large fortune, and now had one of the largest private art collections in western America. They said he had a Dalí. They said he had several of da Vinci's original sketches. They said he'd made his money on the stock market, or as a diplomat for a foreign ruler, or as a Hollywood movie producer, or in an inheritance from a great uncle he'd never known. They said he'd killed a man who cheated him over a poker game.

But, despite what people said, or perhaps because of it, he was a man generally well-liked and well-regarded in the community, although he'd only lived in Mesa Rapids for a few months, mostly due to his free-spirited generosity with his money, and the lavish parties he held, to which everyone in town longed to be invited.

In fact, ever since Harold Klimt had come to Mesa Rapids, people in town had been acting strangely—more foolhardy, more excitable than usual. But that was only the normal course of things when a new and rousing face appeared in town. After all, many wealthy and eclectic characters lived in Mesa Rapids. There were well-to-do horse ranchers and businessmen, artists and art collectors, inheritors of oil fortunes, and several people in the Hollywood movie industry—producers and directors, camera operators and special-effects engineers, and everyone in between—Mesa Rapids's scenic landscapes and surrounding desert being the perfect setting for films ranging from Westerns to otherworldly science fiction, further incentivized by the state's support of the industry through massive tax write-offs.

Most of the wealthiest people lived atop Aspen Mesa, a small plateau, twenty miles across, rising above the surrounding river valley; the poorest, below, where the hobbled houses and trailers clung between the train tracks and the Colorado River, there being no middle class in Mesa Rapids. Below the extravagance—the perfectly contoured adobe walls selected for their muted sandstone color; the horse trails and private parks; the ponds, and brooks, and aspen orchards that blazed stunning colors of orange and red in the fall; ridiculous gabled towers; private pools and fields—the less fortunate congregated. These people were comprised of the usual assortment of maintenance workers, and teachers, and young adults still struggling to find direction for their lives—especially within the artist's community that was a prominent part of the culture in Mesa Rapids. The citizens of "the valley" rarely intermingled with those of "the hill," except for the occasional town meeting or when an art collector took a fancy in an artist and sent a car to drive the lucky individual up the hill to be paraded about as a "discovery," with lazy bravado and condescension.

Which is why people found it peculiar when Klimt, a man with seemingly endless resources, had chosen the Upshaw Mansion—abandoned and dilapidated—in the valley by the train tracks, as his place of residence.

CHAPTER 2
COLIN

"You're such an asshole," Colin Thorne said.

His friend Derek smiled, driving the car. "Why? Because she's your sister?"

"Fuck you."

"If you insist, but I'd rather fuck Stephanie. She has needs, man. Just like everybody. She'd like it."

Colin groaned. "I should have known better than to show you that picture."

Derek chuckled. "Yeah, can you send it to me? The one where she's in the booty shorts? Is she on Facebook?"

"She's fourteen, you horny fuck!"

"All right, all right."

Derek floored the car through a yellow light.

"Are Phil and Bennie still having that party this weekend?" Colin asked.

"Fuck yeah, they are." Derek shifted restlessly in his seat. "One thousand Jell-O shots."

"A thousand? That's a lot, man. They'll never make that many."

"They almost did last time."

"Almost."

Last time, a couple of weeks ago, Colin had watched Derek spew colorful chunks of undigested Jell-O across the bathroom floor before he could help his friend to the toilet. "Shit," Derek had said, his shaggy hair matting on the toilet's rim. "This shit's never coming out." Colin had slumped against the wall, woozy and disoriented. He'd watched Derek retch, spew, retch again. Someone had pounded on the door and Colin had yelled, "Occupied!" from the toilet.

Derek had mumbled, "Yeah, too much…never coming out…"

Colin had laughed, "I think you puked it all up, man."

"No…not that…this dream…every night…this nightmare…"

Derek had been Colin's friend since they were boys—sort of. They'd been in the same first-grade class. They'd walked to and from school together every day, taking turns kicking rocks or pinecones, tightrope-walking the curb, hiding behind bushes to throw snowballs at the girls from their class. The year after that, however, Derek had been in a different class and their friendship had drifted apart. Derek hadn't spoken to him again until they were in high school, Colin being shy and always unsure of himself, spending his time playing video games with his friends, while Derek played soccer and wouldn't have anything to do with the nerd crowd. But in high school, a girl named Sarah had convinced him to try a cigarette and, even though he was shy, Colin would have done anything for Sarah and her freckled nose and her auburn eyes and her curving hips, and had begun hanging out at the "Cancer Pit" behind the school. At first, he clutched by Sarah's side, too intimidated to speak, but when he'd come around the corner one day after science class and seen her sloppily kissing Jack Stanton while Jack rammed his hand up her blouse, he'd been devastated. It had been Derek, who'd been watching him closely from within the smoker's circle, who had taken him aside and said, "Fuck her, man. She's a dumb slut anyway. Everyone knows it."

He began hanging out with Derek again, first smoking in the old Toyota Four Runner Derek had gotten for his sixteenth birthday while they drove around town, then drinking beer stolen from Derek's father's private stash in the garage.

When Colin had turned eighteen, their senior year, Derek had taken him to a place called "The Ice House" and forced him up on stage. Colin had been petrified with embarrassment at the bulge in his pants and mortified for the girls slapping their breasts in his face. He'd been disgusted and fascinated when one of the girls had made a show of launching Ping-Pong balls from one side of the room to the other. He'd been offended at the spectacle, as he'd been taught to be by his Christian parents, although the bulge in his pants had continued to throb, almost painfully, with heat.

When Derek had announced he was going to the state college in town, Colin had decided to go there too; it was the only school he applied to. They'd been dorm mates. Colin wanted to be an illustrator and took an introductory drawing class along with several of the usual recommended/required bullshit classes (like Astronomy and Psychology 101). Derek, as far as Colin could tell, had not chosen a major nor shown any interest in one; Derek rarely attended his classes.

Only a month into the semester, Derek had shown up in their dorm room with a huge duffle bag clinking with bottles—Permafrost, and Goldschlager, and Hot Damn 100, among others. "Go ahead," Derek had said, grinning that shit-eater's grin of his, "open it."

Colin had tugged the zipper back, the flaps on the duffle bag peeling outward like trembling lips, and stared inside. "What?"

Derek nodded his head: "Shrooms."

The large Ziploc freezer bag had been filled with dried and shriveled brown things. Together, they'd passed a bottle back and forth, until they were slurring their words, and had the courage to eat the mushrooms. Derek had gobbled a few and grinned: "Here we go." Colin had chewed them tentatively, like cardboard, but had still taken too many.

The lights had brightened, the colors deepened. The blankets on the beds had begun to crawl down over the floor like creeping slugs. Colin couldn't speak, although he'd been aware of Derek mumbling constantly. It had felt like many hours, sitting in one place, staring around the room. In the early hours of the morning, Colin had looked up and Derek was passed out on his bed. He'd stood, his legs like rubber strands, and tentatively taken a step. He'd realized then that the floor was covered with piles of luminous eggs and that with each step he took he crushed more of those eggs. When all the eggs were crushed, his life would be over. He'd slumped to the floor and cried, as the pastel sun began to fill the room with light.

Not long after that, Derek had been kicked out of school. They'd been at a house party of a friend of theirs, but it hadn't been as big as their friend had thought, and in the morning, still drunk and reeling, Derek had said how funny it would be to fill balloons with flat, leftover beer from the keg. Colin had been too hungover to go with him and heard later that Derek had been caught on the roof of their dormitory tossing his beer balloons at girls as they walked by (just as Colin and he had tossed snowballs when they were kids), aiming for their chests, screaming, "Wet T-shirt contest!" at the top of his lungs over and over.

Derek got a job making sandwiches and Colin stayed in school, eventually taking more art classes and becoming a somewhat skilled painter; he was on track for a graduate program at a nice art school out of state. Colin still hung out with Derek on the weekends and they still partied together.

"Hey, slow down," Colin said. "You're going to get a ticket."

Derek scoffed. "Who gives a fuck?"

It was Saturday afternoon and they were hanging out, driving around, shooting the shit, but Derek seemed, to Colin, more reckless than usual. Derek had dark bags under his eyes, as if he hadn't been sleeping well.

"What do you want to do tonight?"

"I don't give a fuck," Derek said; his eyes looked glassy, stoned.

"We could... Hey! Watch it!"

The SUV didn't see them speeding through the red light and clipped them in the rear-left fender, jolting the car ninety degrees in the wrong direction. Derek's hands flew off the wheel; grunting sounds escaped him, a deep chuckle.

The red truck, which had been accelerating through the intersection, smashed into them head-on. Derek grinned, tried to say something before he died, but his abdomen had been crushed against the steering wheel, and thick, bubbling blood covered his final words.

The first things Colin looked at were his hands, lying palms up in his lap, shaking uncontrollably. He took one look at his friend—jutting bones shiny with blood, steaming, neck wrenched, face turned toward him, grinning hollowly—and threw up. *It's my turn, old buddy,* he thought crazily. *It's my turn to puke.* He gripped the door handle and pushed the car door open. He fell to the pavement, scraping his knees. He stood. He seemed to be unharmed. He blinked. Other drivers were getting out of their cars and rushing toward him.

Chapter 3
ZACH

Zachary Munroe was afraid to get out of bed. He knew there was nothing to fear, but when he pictured his bare and trembling legs dropping down below the covers, down to the cold and gritty floor, and the darkness behind them, he decided it was best if he stayed right where he was. He knew what it felt like, that icy grip circling his ankles; they were only dreams, of course, but sometimes it was difficult to tell.

The problem was, he found it hard to sleep when his father was working late. He'd often lie on his back, in the dark, staring at the crack in the ceiling by the flashes of the lights from the whooshing cars passing outside. He often imagined things wriggling in the cracks, as if pale grubs might hatch free and drop on him, plopping on the covers, their tiny bodies thrashing toward him, leaving slimy trails. And then he'd hear his father's car pulling into the driveway, the slam of the car door, booted footsteps, and the front door swinging open and slamming closed. His father never came in to check on him. He didn't need his father to do that. He only needed him to be home, to be close. Usually, his father was very tired and half-drunk anyway. To the soft clinking of the bottles from the refrigerator door being thrown open and the humming of the microwave, he'd fall asleep.

One time, he'd been at the park with his friend Bud, fully awake when it had happened. Bud and Zach were in the same third-grade class. Bud's real name was Rosebud—his parents being ex-hippies—something out of the movie *Citizen Kane*, but everyone called him Bud. They'd been cutting through the soccer field on their way home from school together when Zach had begun to feel strange, that icy grip falling over his head, squeezing his brain, and when he'd looked around the park, his heart had beat with terror. A woman was by the swing set, pushing a small boy in one of the swings. A couple of teenage boys smoked cigarettes while they practiced slouching to look cool. A man in a bright jacket jogged with his dog. They were all dead—sallow skin and sagging flesh. "What's wrong, Zach?" Bud had asked him through a mouth missing lips and with eyes rolling insanely. Zach hadn't been able to move, could only watch as the jogging man with the dog veered toward him, the dog with matted and missing hair, slobbering blood, gnashing teeth.

And then he'd blinked, and the vision was gone, the icy crust thawing instantly from his head.

He'd never told anyone about his visions.

Sometimes, at night, he'd listen to a train go by on the tracks, its growing roar slowly drowning out the constant babbling of the river, and as it began to pass by on the tracks just behind the house, if he listened closely, he could hear passengers wailing and crying out. Or he'd hear a rusty creaking sound and imagine a lone man going slowly by on one of those old pushcarts: "G'night, young feller." Creaking away.

He sometimes heard noises from the abandoned Upshaw Mansion next door. He'd watched from his bedroom window, seeing curtains flickering. Once he'd seen a bobbing light in an upstairs window. He thought there might be little scuttling creatures living in the house, secretly skittering through the halls at night. He wondered what they were up to. Bud had dared him a couple of times during the day to walk up to the house and go inside, but he'd refused. When Bud had called him a chicken and made rude clucking sounds, Zach had told Bud he'd sneak inside only if they both went together. Bud had scoffed, "Whatever," turned and skipped down the sidewalk.

But now someone was living in the Upshaw Mansion and it seemed like just another boring place. The curtains were always drawn, even during the day, and they never moved. Now he never heard sounds coming from the house.

He heard a car pull up and the engine die, a car door open, and then close—quietly, not like his dad's typical slam. Zach sat up in bed and flipped around so that he was kneeling on the bed and could look out the window. He ducked his head under the curtains.

A man stood in the dirt drive in front of the Upshaw Mansion. He wore black clothes that seemed too big for him, that draped on his skinny frame. His hair was black and slicked across his skull. He carried a briefcase, dangling at his side.

Zach watched him walk stiffly up to the house. He expected the man to knock, but instead the man simply reached his hand out and turned the knob. The man stepped partially into the house, paused. He turned his head, as if listening carefully for something, then smiled, strange lighting from within the house glinting on his teeth. With his free hand, the man made a motion in the air, drawing an invisible circle with his finger, then was gone, the door shut softly after him.

Zach shivered and lay back down. He stared at the crack in the ceiling above his bed. Not long after that, his dad came home, slamming the front door, shaking the entire house. Zach slept, and when he did, unable to repress his imagination even for a moment, he dreamed.

Chapter 4

LAUREN

"It's a pity what happened to Ethan," the woman next to her said. "The way they found him—cold and purple, his priceless jewelry collection stolen."

Lauren Groveshaw sipped her drink and nodded.

"Although he had it coming. Those boys of his..." The woman trailed off, faded into the crowd.

Soft jazz permeated the air. Lauren began another sip, and then turned the glass up, gulping the rest of the drink down. She dangled the empty from her fingers and in a moment it was taken from her. She snatched another from a tray as it swung by.

"Ethan was a cunt," Lauren mumbled to herself as she threaded her way through the milling people.

"Oh, you must go sometime," someone was saying. "He throws the most amazing parties. Not stuffy like these tiresome obligations." The man speaking waved his hands about to indicate the current festivities. "His parties are wild. Carefree." The man smiled at the small circle of people that had formed around him. When the man saw Lauren entering the circle, he raised his glass. "No offense, my dear."

Lauren raised her own glass in return. "None taken." The man's name was Wilson, she knew—an architect, quite wealthy, with an interest in installation art pieces. He owned a house here in Mesa Rapids, but only lived here during the summer months. If she remembered correctly, Wilson was from New York—or was it Los Angeles?

"A few of us should go down there and introduce ourselves," someone in the crowd said.

"I wouldn't bother," someone else said. "I'd be careful to question the motives of anyone who willfully chooses to live in the valley."

"Perhaps he's not as rich as we think."

Wilson snickered. "Oh, you wouldn't say that if you'd been to his house." He turned, so as to give as much of his audience a chance to see him as possible. "He has some very impressive pieces in that house. He's likely a collector—for museums, that sort of thing."

"You don't *know* what he does?"

Wilson looked embarrassed. "Well, you see, I didn't actually have a chance to speak with him…"

Lauren left Wilson to the wolves. She snatched another drink from a passing tray and slid into a corner with her back against the wall. She wondered where Mark, her boyfriend, had run off. She sighed heavily.

Unlike most of her "friends," Lauren had lived her entire life in Mesa Rapids. She'd seen the town grow, and very quickly. When she'd been a girl, Mesa Rapids had been tiny, little more than a scattering of ranch homes, both the mesa and the surrounding valley providing perfect pasture land for the raising of cows and goats and horses. Then, in the late '60s, the town had begun to attract the bohemian art crowd, and, not long after that, the movie industry. The state government, in an effort to bring money into the state, had passed massive tax cuts and write-offs for anyone making a movie in the surrounding area, and Mesa Rapids, known for its scenic southwestern beauty, had been the perfect location for such projects ever since.

Lauren's father, who had owned a ranch and a few acres on top of the mesa, had found himself suddenly in possession of land that was highly desirable and worth a lot of money. He'd sold some of his acreage to wealthy Californians who were moving into the area—building their ridiculous luxury homes— and kept a small horse farm where he began raising and training horses for film and TV.

When Lauren had been eight years old, her mother had been

bucked from a large stallion and trampled to death. It had been a freak accident, but Lauren had never trusted the horses after that. Even now she distrusted them—their large eyes like dark marbles, teeth like grindstones, powerful bludgeoning legs— and her father had never been able to get her to ride, or enjoy the horses as he did.

When she'd turned eighteen, she'd gone to college in New York. She'd returned, four years later, with credentials enough to fake her way into opening her own small art gallery, and thus her adult life in Mesa Rapids had begun—this life of ass-kissing the wealthy and the self-important—this life of pretension.

Lauren sighed, adjusted her dress. She looked up. Across the room, through the swaying people in their low-cut dresses and sport coats wrapping silk shirts open at the collar, through the mumbling noise of voices raised loud by drink, a man she'd never seen before was looking directly at her, unmoving. The man wore a black suit and his face was very pale, hairless. He appeared to be walking stiffly through the crowd as he came toward her.

"It's nice to see you again." The man had no eyebrows, and what she'd mistaken for a bald head was actually black hair slicked against his skull; his eyes were dark, pupils large and encompassing, a slight smile tugging at his lips.

Lauren looked down at the man; he was considerably shorter than her, would have been even if she hadn't been wearing heels. "I'm sorry. I don't believe we've met." She could feel her own smile faltering.

The man laughed, a deep and guttural sound.

Lauren could feel herself trembling. "My name is Lauren. It's nice to meet you."

"I know." The man's gaze, dark and wide, never left hers.

Lauren tore her eyes away, glanced at her drink, raised it to her lips, although her glass was empty. "And yours is?"

"What?"

"Your name?"

"Call me Mr. M." He turned and began walking back toward the crowd.

"Wait…"

The man stopped, turned his head. "Yes?"

"What do you want?"

The man approached her, walking slowly, until his face was inches from hers. Lauren pushed back against the wall instinctively. The man had no smell of any kind.

"Take this," the man said.

Lauren looked down and saw the man was holding a folded piece of paper out for her. She took the paper, careful not to allow her fingers to touch the man's skin. She swallowed, her throat suddenly dry.

"That's it," the man said, and turned away again.

Lauren watched the man fade into the crowd, floating around the corner and disappearing into another section of her house. A moment later, she heard Mark's footsteps dashing down the stairs. He rounded the corner, saw her, and approached. He grabbed her around the waist and swung her around to face him.

"Lauren, my dear." He kissed her. "What have you been doing? You look a little sick. Too much to drink?"

Lauren squeezed her boyfriend. "I'm fine. Do you know that guy?"

Mark let go of her and they stood side by side against the wall. "What guy?"

"He's very pale, dressed all in black."

"Oh, I think I know who you're talking about. I don't know his name. He's a friend of Ethan's. At least, he *was* a friend of Ethan's. What's that?"

"What?"

"That?"

Lauren lifted the folded paper she'd been gripping tightly in her hand. "I'm not sure." She unfolded the paper.

Mark read over her shoulder. "Excellent! I've been hoping we'd be invited. When does it say? Next week?"

Lauren stared at the note—an invite to Klimt's next party the following Saturday.

CHAPTER 5

MADDIE

Maddie's and Jeremy's first time having sex had been with each other. Maddie had wanted to as badly as Jeremy had, but she'd never let him know that. She'd let him fumble off her bra, flopping her breasts ungracefully. She'd let him squeeze them, which she could tell he really wanted to do. She'd lain back on Jeremy's parents' bed and lifted her legs. "Okay," she'd said, anticipating Jeremy touching her, entering her. And he had, sliding in awkwardly, wearing a condom, of course, and she'd watched a funny look come over Jeremy's face, almost disappointment. She'd expected more pain than there was, but there hadn't been much, and then she could feel him spasm, and it was over. He'd pulled out, panting slightly, and slid to the bed to lie next to her. They hadn't spoken. He hadn't wrapped his arms around her. After a minute or two, Jeremy had slunk off to the bathroom to flush the condom and Maddie had sat up. There had been a spot of blood on the blanket beneath her. She'd tried to wash it out that afternoon, but had ended up throwing the blanket away, balling it up and dumping it in a neighbor's trash can on her walk back to her house.

But that had been several years ago, when they'd still been in high school. Now they'd both graduated and lived in a large house at 2115 Hobby Horse Lane, right across from the Upshaw Mansion, with three other roommates, all artists of some sort or another, Jeremy and she included. Jeremy was a sculptor and Maddie liked to paint; she preferred oils. Jeremy had even had his sculptures shown in local galleries, even sold a couple of pieces. Some of the others in the house had had similar success.

Mostly, however, the house was a constant buzz of activity and parties were frequent. Jeremy was always busy, going out with friends, or working on his next project obsessively in some corner of the house. Maddie spent a lot of her time hanging out with the others in the house, when she wasn't working at the coffee shop. She didn't do drugs like a lot of the others, drank a little, but rarely to the excesses she witnessed on a regular basis.

Sometimes she watched Jeremy hanging on other girls through the raucous crowds from across the room. She'd watch him lean in close and say something and the girls would laugh, then one of them would touch him on the knee, or slap his arm playfully.

One night, she'd gone to bed, eventually drifting off to the music and shouting she was so accustomed to, and Jeremy had woken her bursting through the door. He'd stomped right up to the bed, grabbed her, and flung her to the floor. "Why, bitch?" he'd slurred. "Why're you still here, bitch?" He'd smacked her in the face and she'd cried out, stunned. He'd hit her again, but when she hadn't fought back, he'd stood and backed off, stumbling from the room, slamming the door. The next morning, he hadn't said a word to her and they'd both pretended like nothing had happened. A week later, drunk again and staggering, he'd told her how sorry he was. He'd even cried, laying his head on her shoulder. "I'm sorry. I'm so sorry."

Jeremy had only struck her one other time, but that had been a misunderstanding. Jeremy had backhanded her hard enough to send her to the floor. He'd screamed at her while he rubbed his swollen hand. But it hadn't been her fault. He'd thought she'd knocked one of his sculptures over and broken it, but it had actually been Toby in one of his psychedelic fugues. When Jeremy had found out, he'd apologized.

"Did you hear? Rich got a job in Denver," Leslie, one of her roommates, said from across the kitchen table.

Maddie looked up from her soggy bowl of cereal-mush. "Huh? Really?"

Les nodded her head. "Yup. He's moving out."

"What's he doing in Denver?"

"Not sure. Think he's working for his dad. He doesn't want to talk about it."

Maddie shrugged. "Okay." She scooped and swallowed a spoonful of sludge, grimaced.

Les wiped blue-streaked blonde hair from her face. "Yeah, some friend of his is moving into his room, some guy named Colin."

"Cool."

CHAPTER 6

COLIN

Colin groaned. "You won't even be there?"

"Sorry, man, but I have to be in Denver sooner than I thought."

"All right."

"But hey, don't worry about it—those guys are cool. Just have a couple of beers with 'em and you'll be right at home in no time. All right? I gotta go, okay?"

"Okay. I'll talk to you later, Rich."

"See ya." The phone went dead.

Colin dropped his cell phone into his pocket.

The next day he was on the road by eight in the morning. It had been an odd two weeks, just a matter of days since the accident, since Derek had been killed. He'd been in the hospital, but only for one night. Then he'd gone about his life like always. He'd had a large paper to write and a couple of finals. He'd completed them and done everything he needed to graduate college. He'd gone to Phil and Bennie's one-thousand-Jell-O-shot party and he'd been plastered and had a good time. He missed Derek, but in a vague sort of way. He expected to see his name appear on his phone, that voice saying, "Hey, fucker. Did you forget something? Where the fuck are you?" It was as if an eerie fog had descended over his life, smearing the veneer from things, numbing everything he did.

His dreams had been vivid, made little sense to him, yet felt more real than what happened while he was awake. In one dream, he was floating on the rowboat his dad had used to own, rocking in the middle of a small pond, drifting. His dad was wearing a bright orange lifejacket over a khaki fishing vest, sitting turned away from Colin in the other side of the boat. His dad wore one of those ridiculous hats with the large brim in front and a flap of canvas draping out the back to cover his neck—the "mullet hat" he'd called it. His dad was turned away so that he couldn't see his face. He felt a tug and turned to check his fishing line, but it was only a nibble. He felt his dad watching him, eyes boring into the back of his neck. He turned back, but his dad's face remained looking outward from the boat. The boat seemed to have drifted into a small bog; reed-like growths of vegetation grew up and around them, shivering in the breeze. The boat rocked gently. He never saw his father's face. The sky was dark and it looked as if it might rain. In another dream, he was standing at the top of a small and grassy hill surrounded by open fields at night. Somewhere distantly, he could hear the babbling of a river. He thought it might be the same vaguely familiar river from some of his other dreams. Above him, the sky was a deep and hazy purple; below, the grasses swayed like shadows. At the bottom of the next rise, a lone figure walked along the train tracks. The breeze was brisk and Colin shivered. *Can you get cold in a dream?* The figure stopped, lifted its hand, and waved. The figure called out to him, but a sudden gust of wind snatched the words from the air and Colin heard only: "… don't you see?" The figure turned and walked away and Colin watched him and that was all he remembered of that particular dream.

His phone buzzed on the seat next to him in the car. Colin glanced at it. It wasn't a call from Derek; it was a call from his mom. He let it go to voice mail. He was cruising down the freeway. His car smelled like burned coffee and mildewed upholstery. He wiped sweat from his brow. Fuck graduate school, he thought. This was an opportunity he couldn't pass up. Mesa Rapids was known for its art community. He was going to live with actual artists, not pretentious academics, and he was going to paint his ass off and maybe he'd meet a collector and sell some paintings or get a show and get his name out there. It was exciting. He didn't have any reason to stay in his hometown. This was his chance to get out. He was nervous.

There was hardly any traffic. The flatlands and the distant mountains crawled by to either side of him.

When he pulled up in front of the house, a guy and a girl were standing out front smoking cigarettes and watching him. He stopped the car at the curb, killed the engine, and sat for a moment. He took a deep breath and staggered from the car. He left his things and walked awkwardly toward the house.

"Hey, are you Colin?" the guy asked him.

"Yeah, that's me."

"Cool, man. You smoke?"

"Sure." He took the cigarette the guy was holding out to him. The girl leaned forward with a lighter and flicked it alight. He inhaled deeply—let the smoke out slowly.

"I'm Jeremy and this is Maddie."

Colin nodded. "Nice to meet you guys." He took another drag of his cigarette.

Maddie looked at him and nodded back. Her eyes were large and brown, freckles speckling her nose. She wore a tank top and shorts.

"Don't worry about anything," Jeremy said. "We're pretty chill around here. I'll show you around." Jeremy stepped up to the front door and motioned Colin to follow.

Colin was about to drop his half-smoked cigarette to the ground, but Jeremy stopped him. "Don't worry about that," Jeremy said. "Fuck it. Come on in."

Colin followed Jeremy into the house and Maddie followed behind him.

Jeremy had messy black hair and tattooed tree roots crawling out of the sleeve of his T-shirt and down his arm. When he shook hands, Colin noticed Jeremy's skin was dry, rough and cracked. His shirt was stained and his jeans were caked with dried and powdery clay.

The house was simple but with large rooms, single story. Attached to the living room filled with old couches, there was an open kitchen and then a couple of steps down into another living room—what Levi called "the den." Plastered over the walls were classic movie posters—*Gone with the Wind*, *Some Like it Hot*, *Cool Hand Luke*, *Dirty Harry*, and others—along with cutouts from magazines (some pornographic), and scraps of painted canvas and graffiti scribbles. Near the ceiling between the living room and the den, in silver spray-paint, were the words, *You Are What You Are in the Lizard Kingdom*. There was one hallway that led back into the house and to several bedrooms. Colin's new bedroom was at the end of the hall.

"Cassandra and Leslie went to the store," Jeremy said, glancing at Maddie, who had been tagging along silently behind them—she shrugged. "Anyway, this is your room here. Did you bring anything?"

"Just a few things, left them in the car."

"All right. Well—how about a beer?"

The rest of the evening was a hazy blur. He met Cassandra and he met Leslie and he met others, but he couldn't keep their names or faces straight. There were neighbors from the area and friends of his new roommates all around. Everyone was drinking and there was a bong circle in the living room. He drank until the world was spinning.

At one point he found himself in a corner of the den next to Maddie. "So you're Jeremy's girlfriend?" he asked her.

She sipped her pinkish Cape Cod. "Uh huh."

"How long have you two been together?"

Maddie shrugged. "Since high school."

"Damn—really?"

Maddie smiled.

"Cool." Colin nodded, unsure what to say next.

Maddie turned to him; her large brown eyes looked into his, flicked away, then back. Her shoulders relaxed a little, she seemed to decide he was okay. Then she said, "You're a painter, right?"

This was the first time anyone had asked him about his art. Colin grinned. "Oils mostly. I had a few pieces on display in a couple of coffee shops back home and in college. I was going go to grad school, but I just want to paint, you know? I want to really do it. I just need to find a job in town that pays the bills and then I'm going to paint and paint." He lifted his can and swallowed beer that was warm and flat.

Maddie was still smiling at him. "A lot of us here in the house work at a coffee shop just up the road. I can see if I can get you a job?"

"Really? That would be great."

"Not a problem. How about a smoke?"

"Sure," Colin said, and followed Maddie through the throng of people, watching her auburn hair bob, her ass sway.

Later, on that first night, he dreamed he was in a plush bed in a room with black-and-white-checkered tiles and deep purple walls, windowless. He was straddling someone, his arms holding him up, and when he realized what he was doing, he thrust forward. The nameless woman beneath him moaned. He looked at the headboard on the bed, its wood carved with cavorting animals, and concentrated on his movements. When he looked down, Maddie's soft face was beneath him, her eyes closed, her lips moist and parted slightly. Freckles speckled her throat and the top swell of her breasts, which bobbed as they rocked together. Everything was warm and soft. He began to speed up, and Maddie's moaning increased in volume. He arched his head back, could feel her pushing upward to meet him. He blinked and looked and gray and luminous eyes stared back up at him. Sudden terror spilled into him as Derek's face grinned, then that mouth opened and only a sighing sound came out: *ahhhhhhh*. He tried to stop, to pull away, but Derek gripped him and held him close, continued to buck under him. Derek breathed in his ear: *ahhhh…don't you see…ah…what's going on?*

He jerked awake, flailing on the mattress. It was dark and the room was filled with shadows. His head throbbed, pounded painfully. His throat was dry; he needed a glass of water, but he wasn't sure where he was. He closed his eyes against the pain. Against the pulsing darkness, he passed out.

He awoke as light was beginning to creep into the sky, awoke on the bare mattress lying on the floor in his new room. For a moment, he experienced a sickening jolt of vertigo, unsure where he was or what he'd been doing, and then he remembered he was in his new house—he'd been drinking. He sat up. For some reason, an image of Maddie's smile surfaced in his head and he realized, as the room buzzed around him, that there was sadness in it.

He was woozy, still very much hungover. There was a glass of water resting on the floor next to his mattress; he couldn't remember ever getting a glass of water. He reached numbly for it and drank deeply. Then he stood. The room was nearly empty. Besides the mattress, there was an empty and battered shelf shoved into one corner and a shallow closet with one of its accordion doors missing. Lying on the floor, there was his small suitcase and his backpack—everything he now owned in the world. He was still dressed in his clothes from the night before. He walked stiffly to the door, opened it, and crossed the hallway to the bathroom. When he was done, he staggered through the house. A scattering of dirty clothes lined the hallway floor, a pair of bright green panties. In the living room, a bottle of rum lay on its side in the middle of the room, nearly empty, a dark stain soaking into the carpet.

He stepped outside and onto the porch. He could feel the cool and splintery wood through the socks on his feet. Resting on the railing there was an open pack of cigarettes with a green lighter. He took a cigarette and lit it with a sigh. The sunlight creeping over the mountains cast a fresh shine on the neighborhood through a light mist. No two houses were the same; most were in need of a fresh coat of paint, had a dingy, well-lived-in quality to them, huddled close together, with lots of back houses and storage sheds. In the yard across the street, an old Chevy without tires sat on cinder blocks, dark oil staining the hard-packed earth beneath. Birds added their tinkling melodies to the air. The streak of a cat caught his eye and he turned his head to watch it dart beneath a car and realized he was not alone—emerging from the shadows of the dilapidated mansion next door, a figure stepped forward and looked up into the morning light. Seeing the mansion earlier, Colin had assumed it was abandoned, had been surprised when Maddie had mentioned the name of the man who lived there, whose raucous, elitist parties there'd been talk of crashing—this figure, he knew immediately upon seeing him, was Klimt.

Colin considered wishing him a good morning, his hangover having receded somewhat and to set a precedent for his new life about to begin, but decided against it. As he watched, Klimt stretched his arms out in a funny way, as if reaching toward the sun, uplifting his face to soak in the sunlight, to peer across the way, a curious smile tugging at his face—perhaps he knew Colin was watching. Colin turned to gaze in the direction Klimt was looking, at the crawl of Mesa Rapids winding up the hill, and the road switching back and forth to the top of Aspen Mesa, where something liquid caught the light and flared suddenly, then was gone. When he turned back to look again at Klimt, the figure had vanished, and Colin was alone in the cool morning.

CHAPTER 7
ZACH

At night, they looked like mounds of upturned earth. They huddled together, as if for protection, as if for comfort, weathering the storms that periodically roared through the neighborhood, shaking walls and tables so that pictures fell and glasses spilled. Couples in bed clutched each other and lonely children plugged their ears and waited, because you could never really get used to it, how loud it all was. Dogs tied to fences out back howled and gnawed uselessly at their ropes. Dust came in on the makeshift breeze and swirled, smearing the moonlight a dirty yellow. When the storm was gone, and the train had passed once again, people rolled over in the beds of their trailer park homes, drunks grunted in their sleep, and children, like Zach, if they could, drifted back into their dreams.

Except on this particular night, Zach couldn't sleep—not one wink. His father had been in a particularly sour mood, mumbling to himself, running into things and cursing. Zach had hidden in his room and his father had *not* come in to check on him. But when he closed his eyes, it was the face of the Mystery Man, the same man he'd seen entering the Upshaw Mansion at night a couple of weeks before, not his father, staring back at him.

Bud hadn't seen the Mystery Man at first. Even when Zach pointed out the figure standing on the other side of the fence at school, Bud had turned away, shaking his head. "He's right there," Zach had insisted, pushing Bud around so that he'd look. "What's he doing? He's just standing there. He's not moving."

Bud had insisted he didn't see anyone, but something about the way he wouldn't make eye contact made Zach believe his friend was lying. The bell had rung and lunch had been over and they'd had to head back inside.

Bud never believed Zach when he told his friend about some of the things he saw. A couple of weeks ago, he'd been riding his bike along the dirt paths around his trailer park neighborhood, when he'd seen Mr. Dumphrey running toward him. Mr. Dumphrey, who lived just around the block and sold vacuums and appliances door to door, had had something in his hand and had been waving it around wildly. "Run, kid," Mr. Dumphrey had screamed. "The birds! The birds!" Then Mr. Dumphrey had whooshed past him and Zach had been standing there, propping his bike up with one foot, watching the man bolting down the dirt path as fast as he could go. Zach had turned then to look for birds, half expecting to see a great swarm darkening the sky coming closer and closer, but the air was clear and blue; a wisp of cloud, a thin contrail from an airplane, blooming as it dissipated. He'd shrugged, turned his bike, beginning to feel hungry, and headed for home. It wasn't until that night, lying awake in bed staring at the cracks in the ceiling, he realized the thing in Mr. Dumphrey's hand had probably been a gun.

Another time he'd seen a coyote kill a housecat. He'd actually been watching from a copse of rocks in the woods around the river when he'd heard a screech and snapped his head up to see a small wolf-like animal with something orange and furry thrashing in its mouth. He'd heard the crunch of the cat's back and hadn't been able to tear his eyes away from the predator snapping flesh like rubber free from its kill. There had been a lot of blood. When his weight had shifted and a branch had snapped beneath him, the coyote had darted into the foliage, taking its prize with it, leaving dark stains on the leaves and orange tufts of fur drifting about like cottonwood seeds. Bud thought Zach had made the whole thing up.

What he hadn't told Bud he'd seen was a bird flying over the Mystery Man's head that day on the playground suddenly plummeting dead to the ground.

Now he couldn't get out of bed. And he couldn't sleep. He

was frozen, that icy crust wrapping his heart, watching the window, even though the curtain was drawn. If he pulled it back, would he see that face again? Would that grin and those pooling black eyes be right outside? And were there really things wriggling in the dark corners of his room?

He thought if he held his breath and listened carefully, he could hear something pushing against the glass, slimy and moist. He thought, if he were to peek through the curtains, he'd see the Mystery Man with his face pushed against the glass, making grotesque faces, his lips like worms, tongue a throbbing slug.

The next day at school, he saw him again.

CHAPTER 8
COLIN

To get to the coffee shop on the other side of town, they had to cross the train tracks, and the fastest route they could take was along "trailer park road," Jeremy called it. The pavement gave way to gravel and the car ground forward. Jeremy was driving and Colin was in the passenger seat. The car hit a bump and Colin watched Jeremy jostle in his seat.

"She'll get you a job all right," Jeremy said. "Just ask for the manager and tell him you're a friend of Maddie's."

Colin was nervous. In high school he'd worked as a cashier at a hardware store and then in college he'd had a part-time job in the print studio on campus. But he'd never really fully supported himself with a job before. Now he had to pay rent and other things and that was added pressure.

The car pulled up to the flashing lights and the *ding-ding-ding* of a train preparing to pass. "Bullshit, man, these trains," Jeremy said. The train began to *whoosh* by in front of them. "Sometimes you have to sit here for fifteen minutes if the train's long enough," Jeremy shouted over the noise.

"Isn't there a faster way to go?"

"Not really. Most of the town used to be between the river and the train tracks, but now it's all over the place. We have to pass through the shitty part of town to get to the coffee shop. It's right at the bottom of Main Hill Road, that leads up to where all the rich fucks live."

"Huh. Okay."

The thought of working with Maddie made Colin's heart race, even though he knew she was with Jeremy—he couldn't help himself.

The train rattled by and the light rail lifted. Jeremy gunned the car forward, up and over. On the other side, the road was noticeably bumpier.

"Where do *you* work?" Colin asked.

"Here and there."

They were passing along a dirt road lined with trailers. Looking out the window, Colin watched a little girl with pigtails drawing in the dirt with a stick. Sitting on the steps of his trailer, a man with a beard and a greasy baseball cap was drinking a beer from a dark bottle. A woman lurked in the doorway behind him, brushing her hair.

"Hey, I wanna show you something," Jeremy said, suddenly jerking the car down a side road. They skidded through a narrow alley and pulled up in front of a rig painted an old '70s mint green color. Jeremy killed the engine and swung his door open.

"What are we—"

"Just come on," Jeremy said.

Colin unbuckled his seat belt and got out of the car. Jeremy was already jumping up the metal steps and pounding on the door to the trailer. Colin walked up, hanging back a little.

"Yeah?" a woman's gravelly voice came through the door. "What is it?" The door opened and the woman stepped into view. "Oh—Jeremy!" the woman said, her voice softening instantly and excited. "What are you doing here? What time is it?"

Jeremy laughed. "Just showing my friend Colin around. Passing through. Thought I'd stop in."

The woman looked at Colin, her brow furrowing. The woman was in her forties maybe—it was difficult for Colin to tell. Blue eye shadow pooled around her eyes and pink lipstick smeared over her lips, a shade that would have looked childish on someone younger, but that looked clownish on this woman. Her hair was unnaturally blonde, tied back in a bushy and unruly ponytail. "Any friend of Jeremy's is a friend of mine," she said, and when she smiled, there was more of that pink lipstick on all those teeth.

It was smoky inside the trailer, cramped and hot. A cigarette smoldered in a seashell ashtray on the counter in the kitchen area. A curtain of faded plastic beads separated the living area from the entry space. From his spot slumped in one of the chairs at the table, Colin watched Jeremy and Layla (as she'd introduced herself) sloppily making out on the couch, rubbing, lips locked with saliva—desperately, almost violently—stretching their tongues into each other. When they stopped for a second, Jeremy panting by her side, Layla turned to Colin, and began to talk.

"So, are you an artist too?" Colin picked nervously at the label on his beer, his head swimming with the shots of Jack Daniel's they'd already taken.

"Uh, yeah. I'm a painter. I just moved here. I'm Jeremy's new roommate."

"Oh, his roommate. That's nice."

Colin tried not to look: Jeremy's hand had crawled up Layla's leg, was working away under her skirt.

"Working on anything interesting?"

Colin swallowed. "I have some ideas. I just need to get supplies and—"

Layla's eyes were glazed, not really seeing him.

"Maybe we should go," Colin said.

"Hang on," Jeremy said. "Let's have another shot first."

"No, I can't. I won't be able to talk to the manager about getting that job."

"Sure you will. Just one more," Jeremy said.

Colin scratched nervously at the stubble on his cheek. Layla was watching him closely. He was already very drunk. He shrugged. "Fine."

Jeremy laughed humorlessly, grabbed the hair at the back of Layla's head and yanked her mouth toward his.

Colin sighed and turned away.

CHAPTER 9
LAUREN

Lauren lay on her back awake in bed. Mark lay on his stomach next to her, sleeping, tangled in the sheets. Lauren blinked at the darkness toward the ceiling while she listened to her boyfriend's light snoring. She sighed. Something was bothering her. Actually, she knew what it was, but she didn't want to think about it; it was better she get a decent night's sleep. She'd feel better about it in the morning.

She and Mark had spent most of the day perusing the galleries, keeping current on the latest trends, always looking for that hot new artist that she might want to feature in her next column in the magazine she owned: *Mesa Spectrum*. Mark was the current photographer on staff—he took the pictures of the artists standing by their works or posed in galleries with serious looks on their faces and their arms crossed or held out dramatically to show how enthusiastic and knowledgeable they were about their art—and he'd been working directly with Lauren for six months. They'd been dating for three.

For the past week, a dreadful feeling had been growing in her. She'd been questioned by the police on Monday about Ethan's death, but she knew little about him other than that he was rich and supported a lot of young artists (especially young men, but she refrained from mentioning this fact to the police), and he was an investor in her magazine. Then, later in the week, she'd attended a fundraiser for children with AIDS in Africa and been forced to give a short speech about her magazine in front of everyone, which she loathed. And Mark had been excited about Klimt's party. It was all he'd talked about the entire week. He kept telling her things he'd heard. He told her the parties never really stopped, that some people stayed for several days, drinking and laughing through the nights and into the days. He told her he'd heard Klimt had traveled all over the world, collecting artifacts from many different cultures, some civilized and some not. Mark said there was a rumor Klimt had killed someone, but "I'm sure it was in self-defense," her boyfriend had assured her. Klimt was looking for someone, had a big business project in the works—completely confidential—that he needed the right people to help him with. "That's why he came to Mesa Rapids," Mark had told her. "They say he's a high-end drug dealer, but I don't think that's true. Do you? I think he throws these parties because he knows there's someone here in Mesa Rapids that can help him. Who knows? Maybe that's us. Maybe that's us!"

After making overenthusiastic love to her, which she endured passively, Mark had slid to his side of the bed and said, his words already thick with the sleep he was drifting effortlessly into, "Tomorrow, babe. It's tomorrow…" And she, of course, knew exactly what he was referring to. Tomorrow was Friday, and Friday night was Klimt's party. Why did she feel anxious? What was going on? Why did she feel near the brink of impending disaster?

CHAPTER 10
COLIN

"One time," Colin was saying, "my friend Derek went to the blood bank to donate blood and when he was finished, the Band-Aid still on his arm, he went directly to the liquor store and bought a fifth of Captain Morgan just to see how wasted he could get."

"Oh, shit," Jeremy said, slapping Colin on the shoulder. "I bet he got fucking hammered. You're not supposed to drink after that shit."

Colin shook his head dramatically. "No. You're not. I found him a couple of hours later and he could barely stand."

The kitchen burst with laughter.

"So what did you do?" Jeremy asked.

Colin shrugged. "What could I do? I took the bottle of Captain, lined up six shots, and downed 'em."

More raucous laughter.

"You're all right," Jeremy said. "Hey, how about another shot."

"All right. Shots for everybody!"

What could have been minutes or hours later, Colin was sitting on a chair in the corner of the den, smoking a cigarette, watching people funnel in and out of the room. For some time now, a little white, scruffy-haired dog had been staring at him from the couch. The terrier blinked at him through the smoke and from time to time groaned faintly. He could hear people looking for each other, finding each other, making plans, then losing each other again. Some time later Jeremy appeared in the archway, pointed at Colin and disappeared. A young man in tight jean shorts and a midriff approached him. The young man crouched down next to him so that they were face-to-face and said his name was Chris and would he like to buy some drugs? Chris had on eye shadow and purple lipstick. Colin pulled a fifty-dollar bill from his pocket and Chris gave him twenty little blue pills of ecstasy.

In the living room he saw Jeremy punch another guy, breaking the guy's nose. Then there was a great commotion as people rushed toward the kitchen and bathroom for tissues and towels. There was blood all over, soaking into the carpet with a dishtowel over it. He saw Maddie watching him from the hallway and he dropped his eyes and turned away.

"You need a job?" a girl with pink streaks in her hair was asking him.

He nodded, swaying against the wall.

"My daddy owns a gallery up on the hill. Give me a call and we'll get lunch and I'll see what I can do." The girl smiled and her teeth were large in wide-angle up close and the shiny stud in her nose made her nostrils flare like cave openings.

Colin looked down and the crumpled note in his sweaty hand said: *Ashley*, with a phone number punctuated by a pair of hearts.

…He was standing beside Jeremy's bed and Jeremy was sitting up clad only in his underwear with a large portfolio in his hands.

"This one's called Grim Wonderland…Burning Bridge… Luminous Lights at Midnight…Underworld Triptych… Miser…The Bride…Derek's Return…Loneliness…The Crimson Curtain…"

Cassandra and Leslie, two of his new roommates, were laughing ceaselessly from the doorway…

Then he was sitting lonely in his room staring out the window at the mansion next door as the sun once again rose into the sky, wondering if things would ever change, waiting for another day to begin.

CHAPTER 11
THE UPSHAW MANSION

The music began, as it did each week, sometime on Friday afternoon, and people began to arrive long before sunset. Vehicles quickly filled every possible angle of the weedy yard, and then, when that was full, every square inch of the street. Men in suits and women in gowns festooned with sequins marched hand in hand, laughing and talking excitedly, into the shabby mansion. Lights blared from the windows and the music became a constant rumble of energy that rattled the pots hanging in the kitchen and the single-paned glass in the surrounding lower-class houses.

The night before, every Thursday at around midnight, a several-car train stopped its usual route, braking miles before, screeching to a stop, to deliver supplies in unlabeled wooden crates to the back of the mansion. Klimt must get everything he needed this way—personally delivered groceries and fifths of bourbon and vodka, cases of bottled beer, fresh sheets and towels, and all manner of other things—because no one ever saw him leave the Upshaw Mansion, just as no one had seen him arrive.

The serving staff wore purple and could be seen busying themselves as they prepared for the coming festivities. They ceaselessly carried sack after sack of trash out to the back of the house where the train would stop to take it all away, (there being far too much for the city service to manage) and carried the wooden crates into the house to replace what they expelled. They flapped by the windows as they cleaned them with rags and sprays. They swam through the house, dusting, and straightening, and placing tables and centerpieces.

Then, as night fell and the air began to cool, crowds swelled in and out of the house; the front gardens began to brim and spill laughing people into the streets. The house itself seemed to breathe with light and life. The music intensified, and, minute by minute, the past and the future were no longer of any concern. The groups melded and separated like droplets of oil in frothing seawater, until they were one large amoebic mass— except for the wanderers, drunk and cast out, with looks of forlorn misery or, on occasion, understanding terror painted on their faces, before they were once again called back, becoming the brief centers of attention and could forget their worries and the truth of the whole charade of which they may have caught a glimpse. Parties are not places to be insecure with reality.

CHAPTER 12
LAUREN

Lauren selected several dresses from her closet and draped them over the bed. She was trying to decide what she should wear to the party down in the valley. Mark was adjusting his tie in the mirror over the dresser nearby.

"You should wear that one number, the red one," Mark said.

"For a valley party? Really?"

"Mr. Klimt is a very important man," Mark said, sounding as if he knew Klimt personally. "He could be an excellent contact. Maybe he'll even donate to the foundation."

Lauren made a face Mark couldn't see and began looking for her red dress. "The foundation" Mark was talking about was the Art Therapy Foundation for Children with Developmental Disabilities, a non-profit organization she had started years ago to encourage educators to use painting and drawing as a means to facilitate communication with children with disabilities, such as autism.

She took the red dress with its hanger from the closet and draped it next to her other selections on the bed. "I don't know," she said, half to herself. The red dress was formfitting and low-cut. She knew she had a good figure—she didn't like gyms, but she jogged several miles every morning before her usual breakfast of egg whites, toast, and grapefruit—but the red dress was a little too sexy for a stranger's party. She didn't even know who was going to be there.

"Come on, honey," Mark said. "You want to look amazing tonight, don't you?"

"I guess." Lauren sighed. She snatched the red dress from the bed. "Turn away," she said to Mark.

"I don't know why you're so squeamish about these things. It's not like I haven't seen you naked before."

"Never mind. Just let me get this thing on, okay?"

"Okay." She could tell Mark was grinning, but knew he'd respect her wishes.

Earlier, that morning, she'd been awake instantly, sure something was wrong. She'd stepped out of bed, Mark still asleep, and gone to the bathroom. As she'd relieved herself, her heart had begun to slow. What was she so worried about? There was nothing to worry about.

She'd dressed in what Mark called her "yoga clothes," although she only used them for running, and she'd left the house for her morning jog. She'd taken her usual route, down Glendale Street and across to the park that ran behind the houses, then the bike path through the trees. Shielded from view within the foliage that carved a winding tunnel through the neighborhood, she'd begun to feel calmer. She'd picked up her pace, jogging faster, beginning to sweat. Mesa Rapids had always been good to her. As a little girl, she'd always loved the feel of the crisp mountain sunshine on her upturned face; playing in the snow all morning before going inside the house for her father's hot chocolate, the steam defrosting her nose; her father brushing the horses, patting their flanks; letting her feed the chickens that pecked at her feet as she giggled. Then, as an adult, respected for her academic achievements and confident speaking voice, the success of her magazine, surrounded by friends, the nod of her father's head, his proud grin. Mesa Rapids was her home. Why then, these past few months, had it felt strange to her, the air gone stale, the people souring, on the edge, curdling?

A strange sensation had run through her. She'd ignored it, hadn't wanted to spook herself, but she'd felt as if someone were standing in the trees up ahead, someone watching her. She'd stared, her legs beginning to pump faster, scanning the looming green, but could see nothing out of place. She'd been able to see the next turn in the path, which snaked back to the main streets, just a little ways ahead. She'd been breathing hard, getting a good workout.

The sensation had shifted then, become more intense, and she'd run toward the turn in the path. It had seen her. It had come for her. She'd been able to feel those eyes watering with hunger.

She'd flung herself down the path—suppressing the need to look behind her, to see the blur coming after her—hating her fear, knowing there was nothing there, but still unsure, nearly screaming as she burst onto the empty street, still too early for there to be people about—her heart pumping sickly in her chest—and ran the rest of the way home.

"You almost ready?" Mark asked her from the other room.

"Yes, yes," Lauren said, finishing her makeup in the mirror. She smiled at herself. She knew how to disguise her emotions. She looked good. "All right, let's go."

"Damn, woman," Mark said as she came out into the living room, whistling, slapping her lightly on the rear as she passed him on the way to the door.

"You're a child," she said, smiling.

"No, I'm a photographer," and he returned her smile with a grin.

When they reached the party, the crowd was already forming outside and Mark had to drive the car around past the house and park on another block. "Make sure to roll the windows up all the way," Lauren said. "And don't forget to the lock the doors."

Lauren stood on the sidewalk, glancing up and down the street filled with homes that looked to her as if they'd been haphazardly erected on site as temporary structures for a movie set that no one had bothered to film. Still, there were lights on in most homes and that meant there were people here and, although she was genuinely concerned the car might be broken into, she found it somehow comforting to see all those glowing windows, to know that so many people—normal, working-class people—were in such close proximity. "What are you worried about? This is Mesa Rapids," Mark said.

True, she thought, as she took Mark's arm and they began to walk. But it wasn't really the neighborhood that scared her. She forced Mark to slow his eager pace with a nudge. "Heels," she hissed. He slowed, but she could tell it was an effort for him.

When they reached the crowd, people turned to greet them and parted to allow them to approach the house. Immediately, she recognized certain faces. Bruce Summers, known for his southwestern landscapes, nodded and raised his drink. Karen Wintermyer, who trained horses on her father's ranch, saw Lauren looking and came through the crowd. "It's great to see you here," she called. "I wanted to congra—" But Mark still had her arm and she was pulled through the swirling bodies. Most, she was surprised to discover, she did *not* recognize.

"Lauren! Oh, Lauren!" She turned and Maryelizabeth Barker was pushing toward her. "I needed to speak with you!" Mark was still tugging her, but she stopped and pulled away to allow Maryelizabeth to catch up. Mark forged ahead, and she watched him go, dismayed, wondering when she'd see him next, and then his slick-haired head disappeared among the obscurity of the others. "I just have to tell you about this new boy I've discovered."

Maryelizabeth was one of several extremely wealthy art dealers who lived in Mesa Rapids. A few years ago, she'd discovered someone, a young woman who went by the name of Kacy, who painted beautiful blooming flowers that looking like vaginas. For several months after, Kacy's work had spread through town and the larger market, becoming increasingly valuable as demand increased. Maryelizabeth had, of course, taken full credit for her discovery, and had, incensed by her brief brush with fame, been chasing her next big discovery ever since. She was also a generous donator at Lauren's charity events and it was best for Lauren to play nice.

"Oh, do you not have a drink yet?" Maryelizabeth said when she finally pushed her way to where Lauren stood, blinking strangely, as if she'd forgotten what she was so eager to talk about. "The waiters are around here somewhere. Don't move." And then, just like that, she was gone again.

Lauren shrugged, unable to believe her luck, and went in the direction her boyfriend had gone, coming up the steps, through the bustling door, and into the house. She snatched a drink from a tray as it swung by, drank it quickly, snatched another.

She was already beginning to feel better. Perhaps she'd explore a bit. And then she'd find Klimt and thank him for his hospitality, get Mark and end the night with a hasty retreat.

Chapter 13

COLIN

On the front porch, Colin smoked cigarettes with Cass, and Les, and Jeremy, and watched the sheen of the new and luxury vehicles begin to fill every possible angle of their neighbor's weedy yard, and then, when that was full, every square inch of their humble street.

"We should crash," Cass said.

Jeremy huffed. "Yeah right. We'd really fit in with *that* crowd."

"If we dressed up a bit, got out of these shabby clothes, why not?" Les said.

Colin took a drag on his cigarette and looked around at the faces of his new friends. He wondered if Maddie might like to go. He'd spent most of the day with her.

"Fuck it. I'm going," Cass said.

Earlier that day, Colin had asked Maddie when she was going to work and if she'd mind taking him to talk to her manager about that job. He'd told her Jeremy had dawdled, taking him around, showing him the town, but that they'd run out of time and it'd been too late to go to the coffee shop after that. Maddie had given him a strained smile and nodded. "Sure," she'd said, and Colin's heart had leapt.

In the car he'd said, "So, your manager's name is Kim? What should I say?"

"Just tell her you're a friend of mine and you need a job," Maddie had said, turning the wheel of the car with her dainty arms.

Colin loved the way her auburn hair fell across her cheek,

the smooth line of her jaw; the pale stretch of her neck. He'd been nervous and hadn't known what else to say.

When they pulled into the parking lot, Maddie had flashed him a radiant smile, told him not to be nervous, and led him inside.

Unfortunately, the position had already been filled and Colin spent the rest of the day bumming around the coffee shop, reading a random book, drinking the free espresso drinks Maddie gave him when one of the baristas made the wrong drink, and talking to her when he could. He'd learned she was from Denver originally, grew up there. Her father had a good engineering job and her mother had stayed at home taking care of her and her older brother, who was now in college on an exchange program of some sort in South America. Colin had told her his parents were divorced and his dad was a drunk, had used to abuse his mother. He'd even told her he used to have crazy, violent dreams when he was younger, dreams where he was eight years old and had to fight his dad to protect his mom, where his dad grew huge, surrounded by smoke, and fingernails and eyes began to grow all over his dad's body before he charged Colin like an enraged bull. Maddie's eyes had widened as he told her these things, and she'd listened intently, genuinely interested, and she'd smiled sympathetically when he was done—without judgment. Colin felt somehow close to Maddie, as if they'd known each other a long time, that he could tell her anything.

The door to Maddie's room was open. Colin rapped it lightly with his knuckles. "Hey, Maddie?"

She was going through her dresser. She turned, a large smile lighting up her face when she saw him. She was wearing a colorful summer dress that fell to just above her knees. "Yeah?"

"You wanna crash this rich-people's party next door with us?"

"Okay," she said, running her fingers through her damp hair. "I just had to wash the coffee smell out of my hair. It smells good when it's every once in a while, but when it's every day, it really sucks." She wrinkled her nose. "Smells like shit."

Colin laughed. He felt good. "Come on," he said. "I'll wait for you outside."

CHAPTER 14

MADDIE

Maddie shook her hair out straight, brushed mascara quickly through her eyelashes, wrinkled her nose in the mirror, and was ready to go. She didn't wear much makeup usually, had never felt the need to. Jeremy had made a couple of offhand remarks about it once, but she'd ignored him and he'd never brought it up again. She practically skipped out of her room to join the others, stopping herself in the hallway. She was in a good mood—why? She normally wouldn't have felt comfortable going to a party full of people she didn't know, but Colin had asked her and that was good enough for her. She liked Colin. He was fun.

When she stepped into the living room, all the others seemed to be ready and waiting for her. Colin smiled and she smiled back.

"You ready?" Jeremy asked.

"I'm ready."

Cass and Les followed Jeremy outside. Maddie walked next to Colin. "Let's see how many free drinks we can get before someone kicks us out," Jeremy said.

Colin was grinning. "Let's go."

They crossed through the weeds to the sidewalk and walked up the street. Most of the streetlights were dark, but there was enough light from the Upshaw Mansion to illuminate their way on this moonless night. Jazz music filled the air, growing louder as they approached. People filled the yard, chatting loudly with each other, drinking from old-fashioned glasses and champagne flutes. No one looked their way as they turned from the street and began to pass through the crowd, huddling close so they wouldn't lose each other. Already there were people dancing on the tarp that had been laid out over the flat patch of ground closest to the mansion. Speakers had been installed on the outside of the house. The five friends entered the house unchallenged and unnoticed.

CHAPTER 15

LAUREN

After close to an hour spent searching for Klimt, Lauren soon realized she was one of the few guests to actually have been invited to the party. Most had simply heard of the event, gotten in their cars, and somehow ended up here. Even of those she knew, or recognized, few had received an invitation as she had. "It's a party," she heard one man say. "Klimt likes there to be a lot of people here." And unless she found the elusive man, that was, apparently, all the explanation she was going to get.

She couldn't find Mark either. And no wonder: the house was a maze. From the huge entry room, living rooms appeared and snaked in every direction like bedrooms in a boardinghouse, each with its own set of paintings secured firmly to the walls and chandeliers of variously colored crystal. From there, a giant staircase crawled upward to several stories that seemed to at first double the size of the house, then triple it.

She'd been drinking rather more quickly than usual and could feel herself becoming tipsy. When she saw someone she knew, she called out to him. "Ben!" Her voice carried across the room more loudly than she'd intended. But when she reached him and put her hand on his shoulder, the man had had a thin mustache and was not who she thought he was. She turned away, embarrassed. "I thought I might find you here," she heard the man with the mustache say. He was talking to a pair of girls in matching baby-blue dresses.

"Yes, we're here," the girls said together. "Sorry we didn't see you earlier."

"That's all right. I've been looking for Klimt."

"Frankly, I'm surprised you remember who we are."

"You've both dyed your hair yellow," the man said dismissively. "Have you seen Klimt?"

"Never met him," the girls blurted together.

Lauren faded into the crowd. It seemed wherever she went she discovered that most had never met Klimt personally, his name fodder for party conversation and outrageous rumor. She'd heard someone say he'd lived in Spain for a few years. She'd heard he was planning to build a massive museum in Mesa Rapids for art and artifacts to rival the Smithsonian. She'd overheard one woman share with a gasping group that a couple months before, she'd mentioned at one of these parties that it was her birthday the following Saturday. And that next week she'd been delighted to find the party festooned with balloons and streamers and Chinese lanterns and she was sure it had all been for her. There was something funny about a man who would do something like that for a woman he'd never met, Lauren thought, moving on to the next room.

After a while, her head began to spin and she found herself opening a door at the end of a hallway. Her heart stopped, her breath caught in her throat. For a moment, she thought she saw something, something bulging and bubbling beneath the sheets on the bed, staining it dark. Then she was hurrying down the hallway and was consumed once again by the crowd. She found herself going down the stairs, pushing through the laughing people, and thrust outside into the cool night. A tray of drinks floated toward her and she lifted another with her hand. A Wynton Marsalis track she recognized was blaring from the speakers. She made her way out to the dancing area on legs that no longer felt like her own. She downed her drink, stepped out onto the tarp, and could hear the gasps of recognition as she began to dance.

Chapter 16

ZACH

It was especially hard for him to get to sleep on the week-ends, with all that noise coming from the Upshaw Mansion. Zach rolled over in bed. His dad had come home hours ago, had passed out on the couch in the living room like he did a lot these days. When he closed his eyes, he saw the Mystery Man standing in the distance, on the train tracks: "Hello, young feller."

And so he snuck out of the house and crossed over the dark tracks and he was at the party. He wandered through the grounds outside, threading between adults that danced listlessly in circles, with grins on their faces, who didn't give him a second glance. Men and women in identical purple shirts carried trays of assorted drinks through the crowd: glasses of all shapes and sizes, liquids of blue, and green, and red, and milky amber—like walking chemistry sets. The adults drank their drinks and continued to grin and chatter.

Zach found the cobblestone path that led to the front of the house and followed it. He kept his eyes down, concentrating. When he looked up, he was nearly there, the Upshaw Mansion seeming to lean out over him. The front door was open and he could see more adults dancing inside, but something kept him from crossing the threshold, a nagging admonishing voice in the back of his mind: *No*, it said. *Don't!* So he followed the wall and crept around the side of the mansion, crouching behind the overgrown bushes. When he spotted a window glowing with phosphorescent light, he stopped. He tiptoed up to the window, lifted himself, and peered inside. He gasped, blinking rapidly. His heart seemed to stop, to become a heavy stone in his chest frozen with fear. His friend Bud was in there, sitting on the bed talking with the Mystery Man.

"Call me Mr. M," he heard the Mystery Man say through the window, as if speaking to Zach.

Zach ducked back down, afraid he'd been seen, but no one came to the window.

"Where is it?" he heard Bud ask.

"It's right here in my briefcase."

"Can I see?"

Mr. M chuckled and Zach was cold. "Let me open it for you."

Zach heard the click of the briefcase latches popping open. He carefully poked his head up so he could see. Mr. M sat on the bed looking intently at Bud, the briefcase open between them, luminescence from within it basking Bud in a strange, oily light.

"What is it?" Bud asked, breathing heavily, excited.

"This is what I wanted to show you," Mr. M almost whispered.

"Oh," Bud said, and the light flickered and Bud began to scream.

And Zach woke up in his bed, flinging himself from his sweat-dampened sheets, his mouth open wide to let out a scream that never came, and he was terrified to slide the shades aside and to look out his window, to see Mr. M's face pushed against the glass, but when he looked anyway, all he saw was the party at the mansion on the other side of the tracks raging into the night, all those adults ceaselessly dancing not with grins of happiness, but grimaces of despair.

CHAPTER 17

MADDIE

"Where did the others go?" Maddie asked.

"I saw Cass and Les head off to the right. I don't know," Colin said.

They were in the main entry room that felt, filled with people much taller than her, like a vast and turbulent pool. As she fought to stay close to Colin, threading between bodies in suits and dresses, they seemed nowhere closer to anywhere, least of all the other side of the room.

"Where's Jeremy?"

"Fuck if I know," Colin said, then, taking her hand, "Stay close."

Maddie let Colin lead her, squeezing his hand tight when someone bumped into or tried to cut between them. "Here we go," Colin said, pulling her toward him. He bent his head close to hers so she could hear what he was saying. "Check it out—free drinks." He pointed to an armoire pushed against the wall, where he'd finally led her, and a tray of drinks one of the serving staff had left sitting on top. "Which one?" he asked her. She grabbed one at random, a tall glass filled with something blue, and Colin took something green.

"Cheers," Colin said, raising his glass.

Maddie clinked her glass against his. "Cheers."

Her drink was sweet. Colin made a face. "Ugh, appletini," he said, then threw his head back and downed it. "I'll try something else." He took what looked to be a glass of champagne.

Maddie took another sip of her drink.

"Looks like sapphire juice," Colin said.

"What?"

"Your drink. It's like drinking liquid sapphire."

Maddie nodded. "I guess." She smiled.

"What do you wanna do?"

Maddie shrugged. "I don't know."

"We could see if we can find Klimt? I think I saw him the other day, but I'd like to get a better look. See what he's really like."

"Sure," Maddie said. "Where do you think he is?"

Colin finished his drink. "Follow me!" he said, raising his finger and pointing ahead in an exaggerated gesture, taking a step forward, then stopping. "Unless you think we should find Jeremy, see what he's up to."

"No. That's okay. Just don't lose me."

Colin grinned. "Of course not. Let's go."

They both took fresh drinks with them as they charged back into the crowd.

They'd lost their friends, but that was okay, Maddie thought, as they made their way toward the stairs. She'd rather hang out with Colin anyway.

On the stairs, they hurried up, ducking this way and that, until they spilled out onto a landing on the second floor. There were more stairs going up, but Colin hesitated. "You think he's at the top? He's probably at the top. What do you think?"

"Let's check here first," Maddie said, indicating an impressive and important-looking door just down the hall.

They came into a Gothic-style library, paneled with dark, scrolled wood, shelves of books lining the sixteen-foot or so walls from floor to ceiling. More freestanding shelves filled the open space of the large room, interspersed with small round tables and ornately carved wooden chairs. A musty smell enveloped them. *This place is old*, Maddie thought. *It's as if these books have been here for hundreds of years. But that couldn't be right, could it?* The light had a strange quality. Looking up, she saw the ceiling had been painted, a mural of indistinct people, like smudges or shadows, cavorting and looking down on them with flat, featureless faces, lit from the edges of the room.

A slightly overweight, middle-aged man with thick-lensed glasses jumped up from where'd he'd been sitting when he noticed them. He turned to her first, looking down at her legs, lingering, snapped his head up, then turned his suspicious, magnified eyes to Colin. "It's all right here," the man said, waving his arms about.

"What is?" Colin asked.

"In these books. The history of Upshaw Mansion."

Maddie saw the man was swaying, clearly drunk. "Oh, yeah?" she said, trying to be polite.

The man swung around so his face was inches from hers. "Did you know Charles Upshaw had seven daughters and no sons? Drink?" He raised a bottle and offered it to her. She glanced at Colin, who shrugged, so she took the bottle and swallowed, fighting not to choke on the burning liquid. Immediately, she felt drunk. She passed it to Colin, and he raised the bottle to his lips. "Did you know his daughters killed him?" the man continued. "They hung him from one of the rafters in the basement to make it look like an accident. Then they ran away and were never seen again."

"Why would they do that?" Colin said, clearly not impressed and a little amused.

The spectacled man shrugged. "It's all right here." He waved a book he was holding through the air. "There was a tragedy— fifteen years ago. An entire family was found cut into little pieces in the basement. And there's never been a resident since."

"Oh, that's not good," Maddie said.

"And the hum. Have you heard the hum?" The man turned his face up to Colin's. "Only certain people can hear it. Can you hear it? How about you?" He swung back on Maddie.

"Uh," Maddie responded, looking over the spectacled man's shoulder at Colin, who was shaking his head with a smile. "No. I mean, I don't think so."

"Only one percent of the population can hear it," the man said. "Talk to people in town. They'll tell you. There's one in Taos, New Mexico, but there's also one here. I think it comes from this house, I really do. From below. Something underneath. It's all right here—"

"Yeah, okay," Colin interrupted. "We're trying to find Mr. Klimt. Have you seen him?"

The man's magnified eyes blinked. "I was invited. Were you invited? I think most people just come here."

Colin looked at the man uncomfortably and it was Maddie's turn to shake her head and smile.

"I came with my wife. She's around here somewhere. If you see her, let her know I'm in the library. I've been drunk for about a week now and I thought I'd take a break here. Libraries are a good place to sober up. Did I tell you about what I've found? It's all right here—"

"You told us," Colin said. "We have to go."

"Thank you for the drink," Maddie said, unable to keep from smiling.

They left the spectacled man staring after them and closed the door behind them. In the hallway, as soon as her eyes met Colin's, they couldn't contain themselves anymore; together, they burst into laughter. "That was crazy," Colin said, and drew her close and kissed her.

Maddie stood back, stiff, suddenly awkward, unsure what to think, but Colin didn't stop laughing, took her hand, and led her toward the stairs and deeper into the house.

CHAPTER 18

KLIMT

They danced and danced into the night, the crowd, twisting and swirling. Somewhere, from a balcony high above, people knew Klimt was watching, smiling to himself, pleased. The scene had become something meaningful, momentous, profound. It was as if none of them realized they were all going to die.

CHAPTER 19

COLIN

Colin opened his eyes slowly. He could feel the heaviness of the ever-familiar hangover—swollen, but no pain, not yet. He had the sense, as he often did after a particularly wild party, that he'd had a good time, that things had been fun. He looked at the room he was in. His heart began to jolt in his chest. He sat up with a start.

He could remember hallways, and rooms, and people smiling. He could remember laughing and laughing as he led Maddie down dark passages and into dead ends where they had to swirl back and into another room. He could remember a woman in the room with sparkling green eyes saying, *It's good to finally meet you, Colin. It's good to finally know you.* But he'd never seen the woman before and he didn't know who she was. He could remember, in another room, talking with a man for a long time about the painting techniques of the Italian Renaissance—of Bosch and Goya. *I never forget a face.* And Maddie saying, *I'm so drunk. I think I'm drunker than I've ever been.* And her brown and unfocused eyes looking into his as she drew him down, his hands on the smooth skin at her waist beneath her dress. Writhing. Back arching. Her head thrust back, mouth open. Her face coming up. Not her face. But it was. Maddie. Maddie beneath him.

For a moment, the walls seemed distant, obscured by mist, but then he blinked and his eyes cleared and he could see he was in a bed in a small bedroom. The walls were blank and there was a single door, closed, and one window. Crumpled things littered the floor, which he realized slowly were bits of clothing, his jeans and T-shirt like animals run down in the road. The spot on the bed next to him was unkempt but empty. He was alone.

This was a mistake. Please, Colin. Just forget it. Don't tell Jeremy. Please don't tell. And then she'd been gone, sometime in the early hours of the morning, but his head had been too heavy, his tongue too swollen to respond, and he'd been unable to lift himself from his poisoned sleep to go after her.

He stood on legs shaky and numb. He peeled his underwear from the floor and slid it over his crusty and shriveled penis. He gathered the rest of his clothes onto the bed and began to dress. He staggered to the window and looked down. *I must be on one of the upper stories of the mansion*, he thought. He was facing the grounds at the back, the field and then the train tracks. Far below, he could see cars on the road like toys, the trailer park a cluster of geometric lumps, and the city, crawling up the slopes and over the mesa filled with shuddering trees.

Behind him, the door opened with a creek and he could feel the air pressure shift, warm and muggy. "Good morning," someone said. He whirled about.

A man in a navy sport coat stood in the doorway. He stepped into the room, smiling. "I trust you had a pleasant evening?"

Colin tried not to stare. This was the man he'd seen standing at the front of the mansion the other day, who he'd been looking for all the previous night—this was Mr. Klimt. "Yeah," he said. "I'm really sorry to stay over like this. I, uh, should have asked you if it was okay."

Klimt's smile widened. "Oh, that's all right. I thought you might stay over. Lots of people do. It's not a problem."

Colin scratched at the stubble beneath his chin. "Yeah," he said, unsure what he should do. "I'll just get out of your hair." He made a move for the door, but Klimt stopped him with a raised hand.

"I'd like to speak with you first, if that's all right with you?"

"Okay. Sure."

"I'd like to offer you a job."

"You would? What sort of job?"

Klimt's eyes shone brightly. "Would you care for a cup of coffee?"

Colin swallowed. He had no idea what he could possibly do for this man who was dressed so immaculately even so early in the morning. He felt self-conscious in his greasy clothes, head pounding. But still, he did need a job so he may as well hear him out, see what the eccentric old man had to say. "I'll take a cup of coffee," he said.

"Excellent. Just follow me."

Klimt led him out of the room and down a narrow hallway. He stopped them near the end, at another nondescript door. Klimt produced a key from his pocket and fit it in the keyhole, opening the room.

Inside, there was a desk covered with papers, a chair, an old leather couch with a matching love seat, and on the coffee table, a silver platter with an old-style percolator between two upside-down mugs.

"Please. Have a seat."

Colin sank into the couch.

Klimt sat next to him, poured the coffee, and handed Colin a mug. "I enjoyed what you said last night. You have a true artistic mind, if you can only learn to let go."

"Last night?" He tried to remember. "What about last night?"

"You told me about yourself. We discussed artists of the Italian Renaissance."

"Oh, right. Okay." Fragments from his stupor came back to him. Was this the man he'd been ranting to? He could remember standing on a table for emphasis, waving his hands about. He could remember giving a speech in admiration of Bosch's famous triptych.

Klimt was shaking his head. "Yes," he said. "You are exactly who I've been looking for. I want you to paint for me."

Chapter 20
MADDIE

Maddie fled down the stairs, holding her dress down by her sides to keep it from fluttering up shamefully. Her heart was racing. All she wanted was to get away, to hide and be with herself for a while, to get her thoughts and emotions in order. The night before there had seemed to be a lot more stairs, now she was down them and sweeping across the main ballroom and out the door. As she passed through, she looked to the side and saw haggard faces like floating moons watching her from the next room. A man slept in a heap on the floor by the door among discarded cups and kiddie-colored drink stains in the rug.

She couldn't believe she'd done that. She'd never slept with anyone but Jeremy and now she'd cheated on him. And it had been her fault. She'd been the one to draw him close, enticing him until she knew he couldn't hold back any longer, inviting him to touch her, to slip her flirtatious summer dress up and over her head. She had been drunk. She hadn't felt like herself.

And yet, she had to admit, it had felt good. Not the sex part— she could hardly remember that—but the part where she'd been assertive, where she'd done something for herself, something she'd really wanted to do.

She limped down the street. The walk of shame, they called this. She felt gross in the sunlight, tired, sticky. She thrust open the door, and stomped through the house without looking at anything but what was directly in front of her—she didn't want to see anyone, to have to explain herself. She was a terrible liar.

She made it to her bedroom without being seen and closed the door. She sank into the familiarity of her bed.

After last night, she couldn't help but feel connected to Colin, despite her shame, but for a moment things had seemed to glimmer, as if much of what she'd seen last night had not been real, as if there had been others besides Colin, flickering shapes in the fuming light, taking turns as she squirmed on the strange bed.

CHAPTER 21

ZACH

Outside his school, there was a flyer stapled to one of the bulletin boards:

Missing!

Rosebud "Bud" Thompson

Have you seen our son?!

Please call…

Bud looked happy, smiling, innocent, in his class picture from the year before. Identical papers flickered from every light post and stop sign all across town. And only Zach knew what had happened to his friend. He'd seen it, in a dream, in one of his visions, but he knew no one would believe him. His dad knew he had been in bed that night, that there was no way he could have peered through a window of the Upshaw Mansion and seen Bud speaking with Mr. M. There was no way he could have seen the briefcase, and what came from within it. And his dad had told him he'd peeked in on him, had stood in the doorway watching Zach sleep until light had crept into the sky.

Every day at school, Mr. M stood by the fence, but Zach huddled against the side of the building at the top of the hill overlooking the playground, not wanting to get too close. He watched kids crossing the monkey bars, sliding down poles, kicking a soccer ball in the field, chasing each other with giggling faces as they played tag. He watched Mr. M stare at him, unmoving. In class, he began to draw pictures in his notebooks, faces in black pen with dark, spiraling eyes. When school let out, he hurried home, practically running. He needed to find some evidence, something he could show the police so they could go to the Upshaw Mansion and arrest Mr. M for what he'd done to Bud. Maybe if he found that briefcase…

The next day at school, two more kids from his class were missing.

CHAPTER 22

COLIN

Colin was in the rowboat on the river, his dad turned the other way in his orange life jacket and hat that draped down to cover the entire back of his neck. Something tugged at his fishing line and he turned and there was someone calling out to him from the shore, running through the tall grass to keep pace with the boat. He couldn't see who this person was because it was evening and the light was almost gone from the sky. The person spoke, but she was too far away for him to hear, and fell back into the shadows. "Don't you see what's going on?" He turned his head lazily to look at his dad's back. Above them, the sky was purple and bruised. The boat drifted into a slow area in the river, thick with reeds. There was a smell in the air, metallic and unclean. "Hey, fucker. I asked you a question." The figure in the boat turned to him but it wasn't his dad, it was Derek, giving him that shit-eater's grin. The boat rocked in the viscous sludge. The smell grew strong and he could taste it in his mouth, sulfur coating his cheeks and his teeth. The boat bucked as Derek leaned back and forth, laughing, threatened to spill him into the river made of blood.

And then he woke up.

He must still be worked up about Derek's death, Colin thought, sitting up on his mattress on the floor in his room. Even though he'd moved on and had a new life now, his old friend still haunted him.

He stood and stretched. He rubbed the sleep from his eyes. Mr. Klimt wanted him to start his new job today, but he was still a little unsure about what he was supposed to do, if he should take the job. Mr. Klimt wanted him to paint, to make something grand and artistic, but Klimt couldn't give him any direction or suggestions, that was part of the project. It had to be Colin's creation, whatever it was supposed to be.

He went outside on the front porch for a cigarette. Jeremy and Cass were already there. They both nodded at him as he joined them.

Jeremy watched him closely. "You and Maddie have been hanging out a lot."

Colin took a drag, acting casual, talking through the smoke. "I told you; we're just friends."

"Whatever, man."

Colin and Maddie had talked and neither of them could remember exactly what had happened at Mr. Klimt's mansion so they'd decided to forget about it; they'd both been drunk.

"Hey, you guys wanna do something after this?" Cass asked.

"I'm starving," Colin said. "Wanna get something to eat?"

Jeremy huffed, dropped his cigarette butt and crushed it with the sole of his shoe. "You have money for that? When are you gonna get a job?"

Colin shuffled his feet. "I have a little money. I'll get a job soon."

"We can't keep covering your ass, you know."

"I know. I'll figure it out."

"Don't worry," Cass cut in. "We'll help you out if you need it. That's what we do here. We stick together."

Jeremy lit another cigarette. "Yeah. That's what we do here." He didn't sound convinced.

CHAPTER 23

MADDIE

That night, people came over to their house, as they often did, and Maddie found herself engulfed in another party in the middle of the week. A few weeks ago, she would have shut herself in her room and done some sketching or messed around on her computer, but now, because of Colin, she liked to tag along with him, although this inevitably caused her to drink much more than she liked.

She'd had a good talk with Colin and they'd both decided never to tell anyone about that night at the Upshaw Mansion. After a few days, she felt better about it. Jeremy was never going to find out and that was good. She wasn't even sure they'd done anything, not for real. And Jeremy had been nice to her recently and they'd gone out to eat a couple of times. She'd even been staying in his room and they'd made love in the middle of the night, the faint midnight lights glimmering in their eyes, illuminating their skin. Colin was a good friend and he was fun to hang out with, but Jeremy was her boyfriend.

In a corner of the den, surrounded by people drinking and talking in increasingly loud volumes over the hip-hop music Jeremy liked to play, Colin seemed more excited than usual. He was blabbing ceaselessly to her.

"We should go there, we definitely should. That would be so much fun. I'd like to see more of the town. It's really nice on top of the hill. I've never been camping before. Can you camp up there?"

She shrugged. "I think so."

"Oh, okay, we should do that then. It'd be fun. Do you mind if I smoke in here?"

"Other people are."

"Cool," Colin said, lighting the cigarette he'd been rolling between his fingers for the past twenty minutes. "Do you want one?"

Maddie began to shake her head, but stopped. She thought Colin had offered her a cigarette, but he held something else in his palm. "What's that?"

"Ecstasy," Colin said, smiling widely. "You don't have to. It's just that I did one earlier and now I'm really starting to feel it. It's good stuff."

"I don't think so."

"Okay," Colin said, unconcerned, shoving the pill back into his pocket. "I don't even remember when I got 'em. Not really." He laughed. "Some guy at a party here gave me a really good deal. I gave a couple to Les and Cass earlier and to Jeremy too."

Maddie nodded and finished her drink. "Need another drink?"

"Sure," Colin said, standing abruptly, swaying. "Whoa. I can really feel that shit now."

"Stay here. I'll be right back."

Maddie crossed the room. When she looked over her shoulder, Colin had sat back down, his hands kneading at the couch, looking around with glazed eyes.

She moved toward the kitchen. She glanced through the crowd. Jeremy was on one of the couches talking with a couple of girls she didn't recognize. She entered the kitchen to get herself and Colin drinks.

As she came back through the doorway, a drink in each hand, she froze. Jeremy was kissing one of the girls. He was moving his head around sloppily, letting the girl suck on his tongue. She turned away, hurrying through the crowd to get out of sight.

When she got to Colin, she was shaking. She set the drinks down on the end table and sat down next to him. Colin had slumped into the couch and was grinning childishly at her. "Would you like one?"

"Yes," she said. "Yes, I would."

Colin sat up a little. "Are you sure? You don't have to."

Maddie looked into Colin's eyes. "I know. I want to."

"You can have as many as you want," Colin said. "For you, anything."

"I guess I can speak openly now, because we're... you know..." Colin said to Maddie, sitting on the bed behind her, kneading her shoulders with his fingers.

She leaned forward, sighing and rolling her neck.

"Yes, you can."

"It's good to know you," he said, awkwardly, but confidently intoxicated. "You're very pretty." She moaned beneath his fingers. "I don't think Jeremy is good for you. We just...fit better, you know. We—"

"Kiss me," Maddie said quickly.

Maddie leaned her head back and Colin bent down so their mouths could meet. Then he came forward and their tongues were twisting deliciously and she could feel his body pushing against hers and they each gripped the other tight and gave themselves to the drug and to each other.

They were on the bed rolling and undressing when the door slammed open against the wall and Jeremy burst into the room, red-eyed and trembling. "You piece of shit!"

Colin barely had time to sit up before Jeremy came at him. He blocked Jeremy's first swing, but took the second in the ribs.

Maddie was slow to react, the drug making her sluggish. She screamed at Jeremy to stop, then flung herself at him. Jeremy pushed her back. She lost her balance and thudded awkwardly against the frame of the bed. Hot color exploded before her eyes, dark spots dancing.

Then Colin was on the floor and Jeremy was crouched over him, beating him with his fists.

CHAPTER 24
AUREN

"Doctor's orders," Lauren said, placing a healthy breakfast of egg whites, toast, and grapefruit on the table before her dad.

Her dad grumbled. "Any butter?"

"I'm afraid not."

"Jam?"

"No, Dad. As long as your daughter does your grocery shopping for you, this is the best you're going to get."

Her dad made a hard tapping sound with his toast against his plate, trying to make a point, then took an unenthusiastic bite and sighed.

"We have to keep your blood pressure down, don't we?" Lauren said. "You have a lot of good years to look forward to."

"Yeah. Years and years of this shit—cardboard and soggy egg substitute from a box." He looked up at Lauren, giving her the pathetic puppy-dog look.

Lauren returned the look. For a moment, they held strong, looking at each other, until they both lost it and laughed, easy and comfortable with the old jokes.

"How's the magazine going?" her dad asked.

"It's going. Busy—busy."

"And that boyfriend of yours? What's his name?"

Lauren gave her dad a look. "Mark. His name is Mark. You know that."

Her dad forked egg substitute into his mouth. "Yeah, sure. Mark. How is he?"

Lauren smiled. "He's good, Dad. We're, you know, taking things slow."

"Uh-huh." He shoveled another forkful of egg into his mouth and chewed. "Bacon may be bad for my heart, but this shit is bad for my soul," he said and grinned.

Lauren smiled at her dad. It felt good to be home—the stress of her busy life seemed to melt away whenever she visited her dad at the ranch, even if just for a short while.

Before the day warmed up too much, she and her dad took a couple of the horses out for a short trot along the trail.

It was a beautiful day, the sky clear, the sun shining—perfect weather for riding. But the horses, in their stalls, had been more restless than usual. Reba, usually one of the calmest, a small filly children sometimes rode, had been pacing her stall, shaking her head, and huffing. And Hero, a black-haired stallion who had been featured in the western flick *One Last Ride*, had been biting the bars. Even Gerome and Josephine seemed overeager and impatient as they had saddled them each for their morning rides.

Although Lauren had hoped to go on a slow, calming trot with her dad, the horses seemed intent on a near gallop, taking the usual path, the coniferous trees and aspen whisking by.

"Whoa, girl," she said to Josephine. "Whoa."

When they reached the woods, the horses slowed a little, seemed calmer once they were out of sight of the ranch.

After that, they had a nice time, but took the short route back to the house rather than the long trail around the entire ranch. They returned to the barn, gave each of the horses a carrot, and went back inside the house.

Her dad wasn't talking much. Something was bothering him. Something was bothering her too, but she couldn't put her finger on it. Maybe she was just projecting her anxiety over how she'd felt at Klimt's party at the Upshaw Mansion the other night.

A few minutes later, all of her self-assurances, all peace and calm on the ranch, shattered.

"Mr. Groveshaw! Sir! Come quick!"

One of the horse trainers pounded on the door. Lauren answered it.

"Oh, Lauren."

"Hugo," Lauren said. "What is it?"

"Come quick," Hugo said.

Lauren glanced at her dad and he shrugged. They followed Hugo outside.

"It's Joe," Hugo said. "He's been hurt."

When they got to the barn, several of the ranch hands were huddled around someone lying in the dirt. No one was talking, shaking their heads, somber.

Lauren's dad stepped forward, pushing his way into the circle of bodies. He froze; Lauren could see his body tensing.

"It was Gerome, sir," Hugo said.

Lauren came forward.

"Wait," her dad said. "You might not want—"

Joe's body was motionless, the ground dark with blood.

"Joe was feeding him, sir, and…and Gerome kicked him," Hugo said.

"Someone call an ambulance," Lauren's dad said.

"What's that, sir?"

"Ambulance! Call a fucking ambulance, will ya?"

"Yes, sir. Right away, sir." Hugo ran back toward the house.

"What the fuck…" Lauren said.

They all stood, staring. No one said a word.

After a minute or two, Brock, the elderly gardener, his eyes having never left the body, said quietly, "Ain't got no face left."

Lauren shook her head.

Later, after Lauren had left for the day, the horses either escaped, charging headlong into the woods, or died from fright in their stalls, and Hugo fell asleep in the chicken coop with a marijuana joint and he and all of the chickens were burned alive, and something truly horrible happened at the ranch and no one, including Lauren's father, survived.

CHAPTER 25

COLIN

"How could you do this? And with this motherfucker? Really?"

"I..."

"Shut up, bitch! I should—"

Colin could see it in his head. Jeremy throwing his fists out, lunging forward, but stopping himself just before contact, Maddie flinching back, scared.

"Fuck! I just...how the fuck could you do this to me?"

Then Maddie, almost a whisper, "I...I saw you..."

"What? I can't do this. I can't *do* this!"

Colin watched Jeremy stomp from the room through slitted eyes. He watched Jeremy slam his fist against the door frame. He heard Jeremy swearing as he traveled down the hallway and back to the party. He left a smear of blood on the manila paint.

"Colin? Are you okay? Colin?" Maddie said, instantly by his side, her hands on him, shaking him gently.

He groaned. His face was hot. He winced, lifting himself. His ribs felt bruised and puffy beneath his right arm where Jeremy must have kicked him. He leaned on the floor with his back against the bed. "What the fuck..." The drug wouldn't let him be anything other than stunned.

"I'm sorry, Colin," Maddie said, cradling his head, his vision spinning. He let Maddie help him onto her bed, his eyes closing. "I'm so sorry."

When he awoke, his body aching and distant, Colin was alone in

Maddie's bed. He raised himself. With his fingers he delicately explored his face. One of his eyes was swollen nearly shut. He was sore all over his body and his thoughts were numb—the drug had left him with an uncomfortable empty-shell feeling, as vaguely familiar as his memories of toddler years in the muggy heat.

He staggered from the room and down the fuzzy hallway. He wore his sagging jeans from the night before, but no T-shirt. The carpet felt unnaturally spongy beneath his bare feet. His mouth tasted as if he'd been inhaling bug dust. He limped across the living room toward the kitchen.

Les was sitting at the table, looking around as if surprised by the mess, her blue-streaked hair hanging limply from her head. When she saw Colin, she jumped up and ran to him. "Colin, my god! Are you okay?" She began looking over his face carefully.

"I'm okay."

"Are you sure? Is there anything I can do?"

"No, it's all right."

"Here. Sit down. Sit down." Les pulled a chair out for him. "Tell me what happened. Jeremy took off last night and no one's seen him."

"I…well…Maddie and—"

"I knew it!" Les smiled widely. "You and Maddie!"

"Yeah, we—"

"Shit," Les said. "Jeremy is never gonna forgive you." She shook her head. "He's a pretty cool guy most of the time, but he's also the jealous type—he'll kill you for messing with his girl."

"But he's cheating. I saw—"

"He doesn't give a shit about that," Les said. "He sleeps around a little—sure. But he's been with Maddie since they were in high school together. He loves her."

"But—"

"I don't get it either. You're way better for Maddie than he is."

"Yeah, thanks. Where is she?"

"She's in your room with that little dog someone left here. She said she wanted to be left alone."

Colin stood.

"Whoa, hang on," Les said. "You sure you're okay?"

"I told you—I'm fine," Colin said and staggered out of the kitchen.

"I'll find you later," Les called after him. "I have a few painkillers leftover from when I had my wisdom teeth out that should help."

In the hallway, he realized how exhausted he was. He needed rest, but he had to talk to Maddie before he did anything else, make sure she was okay. He should have known to check his room first.

He knocked on the closed bedroom door.

No one answered, so he turned the knob and slowly pushed the door open.

Maddie was sitting on his mattress on the floor, the tiny white terrier curled up in her lap. She looked up at him when he entered, eyes puffy, her cheeks unevenly red. "Hi," she said, her hand absently stroking the sleeping dog.

He stopped awkwardly in the middle of the room. "How are you?"

"Okay."

"That's good," he said, unsure how to proceed.

"Jeremy's such a jerk," Maddie said. "I'm sorry he did that to you. I wish I could take it back."

"Don't worry about it."

"He's going to kick you out if you can't pay the rent, you know."

"Yeah, I know." Colin shifted his weight from one foot to the other. "I need to find somewhere else to live now; not sure where I'm going to go. I'll leave you alone if you want." He turned to leave.

"Don't go."

Colin sighed. He walked over and sat down on the mattress next to Maddie. He slumped.

"You don't have to go. As long as you pay your rent. It was just a drunken fight."

"If I did get a good job and found a different place, would you come with me?"

Maddie gave a canted smile.

"I mean it. Would you come with me?"

Her eyes dropped to the dog. "Maybe."

Later that day, after a couple more hours of sleep and a shower, Colin walked over to the Upshaw Mansion and accepted the job Klimt had to offer him (whatever it was), on the condition he be paid in advance. Colin gaped as Klimt smiled and counted out twenty crisp one-hundred-dollar bills into Colin's open hand.

"You start immediately," Klimt said. "It's best if you work here. I'll be checking on your progress."

CHAPTER 26

ZACH

When school let out, Zach hurried home to dump his backpack in his room. He grabbed a flashlight from one of the drawers in the kitchen, slipped into his back pocket the Swiss army knife his dad had gotten him for his birthday last year, and was out the back door walking through the weeds. Mr. M had been at the edge of the playground like he was every day, in the exact same spot, maybe smiling—like Mona Lisa from one of his textbooks—following him with his eyes.

When he reached the slanted dirt hill that led up to the train tracks, he stopped, listening for an approaching train, feeling for vibrations in the earth. He didn't like crossing the train tracks. He knew other kids who liked to walk along the tracks, but he always imagined that as soon as he stepped up onto them there would be a train he hadn't noticed, coming at him, horn and lights blaring, and he'd leap out of the way and almost make it, but the train would catch his legs and tear them off and he'd be left bleeding in the dust. He looked both ways, took a deep breath, and ran, up the hill, leaping over the tracks, and down the other side. He stomped his feet down to stop his forward momentum and smiled. He didn't really believe a train would hit him. But now he was on the other side and safe.

By the time he reached the road he was thinking how smart he was to bring the flashlight even though it was still light out; it might be dark in the house, even with all those windows. He cut between houses a little ways up the street and trudged through the undergrowth behind the fences. A dog barked and snarled through a crack only inches from where he walked, but that was just Reggie, the black lab, and he ignored the dog and kept going. When he reached the back of the Upshaw Mansion, he ducked through one of the larger tears in the old chain-link fence that marked the border of the property. He stayed where the trees grew thickest—a small, untended orchard—treading through the fallen and shriveled fruit.

He came upon some bushes overgrown by vines with little orange flowers, bright like poison—great tangles of foliage. He could still see the house, blocking the sky like the bulk of an ancient and long-grounded ship, its windows dull, gray despite the clear and sunny skies. For a moment, it was as if something crawled over his shoulder; he brushed at it and turned: was he being watched?

He scanned the trees. There was nothing. Then something rustling the branches, coming into view, but it was just a bird; another magpie, scavenging—its beady eyes like glistening plastic that could be looking at him or anything else in the garden—among the rotten fruit.

Then he was following a narrow cobblestone path and came out into a small courtyard, a dried and crumbling fountain at its center. He hadn't known all this was here. Why hadn't he, in all his time spent exploring alone, ventured into the yard behind the Upshaw Mansion? As abandoned as it was for years, he'd never really believed what the other kids had told him. What had Bentley, a kid from school who lived in his neighborhood, said last year, only a couple of months before Klimt had moved in? *I don't even believe in haunted houses and that place is haunted.* More vines crawled over the long-dead fountain, hanging with some sort of black fruit he'd never seen before, fruit that appeared to bloat as it grew until it split and dripped sticky sap over the stone, stained purplish in places. Inside the fountain, there was only sand.

A little ways farther on, he came out into a large open area, which dipped into the earth, murky with water at its bottom. A small pond? No—it was rectangular: an empty swimming pool. Ornate tiles that may have once been blue peered through the moss and foliage every few feet, and he was careful to follow the path skirting its edge so he didn't slip.

Finally, he reached the back of the house. He thought he could find the window where he'd seen Mr. M with Bud on the bed, opening the suitcase, something splattering out. But it was on the side of the house and he was still at the back. He crouched against the wall to catch his breath, flashlight in hand, and there was a small statue of a little girl behind the bushes, rivulets carved down her stone cheeks from water dripping off the roof like tears. He trampled the leaves with his feet, around the stone girl, and when he came to a window, he stopped. Slowly, he lifted his head to see inside.

From an inch or two between the closed curtains, he could see through the shadowy room to another door, ajar, leaking light. He strained, closing one eye and moving his head back and forth, but could see little else. He gave up and moved on to the next window, but couldn't see much in that one either.

He came to the corner of the house. He had a choice: he could either continue around until he found the window where he'd seen Bud and Mr. M—except he wasn't sure which window it was now or if he was even on the right side of the house—or he could double back and go inside the back door. He turned back.

The door opened easily, it wasn't locked. He stepped inside the house. He closed the door behind him. Immediately, he noticed a shift in the air; it was different, warmer, thicker. He turned right and began to creep down the hall. The light was muted, like the inside corner of an antique shop, where the still-unsorted junk was piled high, obscuring the windows and swinging lightbulbs above. He was glad for his flashlight, but it hardly penetrated the dust. He walked carefully. He was pretty sure he was going in the right direction. He'd seen Mr. M pull the suitcase out from under the bed. If he could find that room... Laughing. Somewhere, someone was laughing, seeping through the house, old wood creaking, the creaking of approaching footsteps. He hurried down the hall. To either side of him, there were doors. It was impossible to know which was the right one. The footsteps were getting closer. He chose a door and flung himself through it.

He stood, his back against the door, listening, trying to

control his breathing. The footsteps creaked— and continued past.

He took a deep breath. He was in a game room of sorts. There was a pool table and a pair of dartboards on the wall. On one side of the room there was a bar, a single row of bottles reflecting into many in the slanted mirror. The crimson curtains were drawn shut. There was another door behind the bar.

He walked around the room, pointing the faintness of his flashlight at the paintings on the wall. One showed a little girl peeking under a bridge. Another depicted a tree with an old man's face. He could hear the creaking footsteps again, stopping outside the door—the door beginning to open.

He ran for the closest hiding spot, diving behind an ancient radiator protruding from the wall. His heart was beating in his throat.

Laughter entered the room. From between the radiator tubes, he watched a man and a woman spin across the rug, clutching each other, until they came to rest against the pool table. Their faces were inches apart and they were both still chuckling. Then they kissed and Zach could hear their mouths, wet and sloppy. They made mumbling sounds into each other's throats, as if still laughing, while their heads moved around and side to side. The man's hand was under the woman's blouse, roving around beneath the cloth.

While the man and woman were distracted, Zach crawled out from his hiding spot and slunk—crouching his head, trying to be as quiet as possible—toward the bar, ducking behind it. He peeked his head up, terrified of being seen, but the man and woman were intent on each other. He watched the man slip the woman's panties down her legs from beneath her skirt where they hung dangling from one of her ankles. Then the man produced a large, uncircumcised penis that looked sickly yellow under the hanging light above the pool table.

Zach turned away, disgusted. He wondered if he should wait until they were done. He had to admit, part of him was curious. He'd heard his dad having sex with some of the women he occasionally brought home late at night—bedsprings creaking, strange animal grunting—but he'd never seen the actual act performed. He wasn't sure he wanted to.

He began crawling toward the door behind the bar. If the man and woman looked up, they would see him opening it, but they were distracted—enough, he hoped, not to notice him. He reached his hand up for the knob, grasped it, and the door opened suddenly, on hinges as if greased. For a second, he feared the door might make a sound, but he didn't hear anything.

All he could hear was, behind him, the grunting beginning, the dog-panting.

He slipped through the opening into a dimly lit room. Slowly, he pushed the door closed until it latched. He took a couple of steps forward, looking around. The room was empty, larger than the one he'd left behind, devoid of all furniture. The walls were bare, the ceiling blank. The only source of light was coming from a single window. There were no other doors.

Zach walked over to the window. He pulled the curtains open with his hands and gasped. Distantly, he watched a train go by on the tracks. A car was waiting on the road for the train to pass like a toy. The back garden was a dark patch of trees, clouds drifting in the sky. He hadn't gone up any stairs, or been lifted in any elevators he was aware of. He'd thought he was still on the first floor, but here he was looking down, seeing the meager corner of Mesa Rapids he called home from many stories up. For a moment, he felt dizzy and wheeled back, tearing his eyes from the window. He sat, closing his eyes, trying to recover his equilibrium. And that's when the tingling began; a crust fell over his head like an icy crown.

Hello, boy. I want to show you something.

Something shifted in the dark.

But when he turned, expecting to see Mr. M standing in the doorway, what he saw instead melted the ice from his mind and froze his heart.

The man from the other room was standing there, completely naked, his penis still partially erect and glistening, grinning widely, chuckling a little but getting louder, until he was laughing again. Still laughing, the man licked his lips and turned and walked slowly back into the game room. Zach could hear the woman laughing too, but he had nowhere else to go, so he stood, gripping his dead flashlight like a weapon, and followed the naked man.

Another time, then.

Putting the small bar between him and the man and the woman, he edged around the room, trying to get closer to the door. He watched the man walk back to where the woman still sat on the pool table with her legs spread, and the man slid his penis beneath her skirt and began to thrust into her. The man never took his eyes off Zach. The woman's eyes were also fixed on him. Their faces turned as he scraped along the wall, following him, laughing the entire time, laughing and laughing.

He felt something stab at his upper back and realized it was the doorknob. Unable to rip his gaze from those four blank eyes, he fumbled with the door, pulled at it; opening a crack, then thudding closed. He pulled at it again; he thrust himself at the crack, beginning to wiggle through.

The man lifted a ball from one of the pockets on the pool table and—still laughing, still looking directly at Zach—smashed it into the woman's face. Teeth crunched dully but the woman continued to laugh and stare and Zach lost hold of his flashlight and was through the door and running down the hall.

When he reached the end of the hallway, a man with one eye stepped out from around the corner and, with a humorless smile, snatched him up tight.

CHAPTER 27

MADDIE

Having called in sick to work, Maddie took her new dog—Isabel, she'd named her—for a walk, and by the time she got back to the house she was feeling better. Isabel hopped up the front porch steps and waited by the door, looking up at Maddie expectantly, tongue exposed happily out one side of her mouth.

Inside, the house was quiet. Everyone must have left, because there were no voices from the kitchen. Even the usual sounds from Toby's room were absent. She called Isabel to follow her and walked down the hallway. She opened the door to her room and closed it behind her and Isabel.

She sat on the bed. A second ago, she'd been feeling refreshed, but now, in this house, the familiar anxiety was beginning to settle over her again. Maybe Colin was right and she should get away. Maybe she should forget about her conflicting feelings and think rationally about her situation. Maybe she should break up with Jeremy and move on with her life, but there were so many uncertainties.

Maddie laid her head back on the bed. Isabel jumped, hung for a moment on the edge of the bed, and then managed to scramble up, turned twice, and plopped down with her warm little body snuggled up against Maddie's. Maddie closed her eyes.

It was a muffled thump that woke her—and splitting wood. Sour skin and alcohol breath filled her room. Isabel began to bark. "You bitch," she heard him say, and then something struck her before she was aware she was even in danger. She opened her eyes to Jeremy's bloated face: eyes red and unfocused, sneering white lips, flushed and blotchy skin. He raised his open palm and brought it down. Maddie blocked the strike with her arms. "Bitch," he said again.

"Jeremy! Stop! You're drunk!"

Somewhere, Isabel barked frantically.

Jeremy mumbled something else, spit flying from his lips, and raised his hand again. Maddie kicked her leg out and felt it connect with something soft. She heard the air go out of Jeremy's lungs and he stumbled back, falling on the floor.

The fight was over. Maddie sat up on the bed and watched Jeremy struggle for oxygen. Isabel was circling him, yapping and growling. "You can't do that, Jeremy. You can't do that anymore."

Slowly, Jeremy staggered to his knees. When he looked up, at first all Maddie could see was hatred, then his eyes cleared, softened, and his face sagged. "I'm sorry. It's always been you, Maddie. Please."

"Get out," she was surprised to hear her lips whisper.

Jeremy stood suddenly. "Fine." His fists clenched at his sides.

"We'll talk later when you're not drunk."

Jeremy crossed the room, Isabel chasing him, barking and jumping about. When he reached the door—its doorjamb splintered and hanging—he turned back. He looked down at the dog, his eyes so red they shined, and raised his foot.

Maddie lunged to her feet, a "no" lodged and stuck in her throat.

For a moment, Jeremy's foot hung threateningly in the air, stomping down, Isabel barking and barking but unaware of her danger.

Jeremy stopped himself. He turned and left.

CHAPTER 28

COLIN

"Okay, okay. It's okay," Colin said, holding the boy, trying to calm him.

The boy looked up at him, terror in the boy's eyes, but he stopped struggling.

"How'd you get in here? Did you come with someone?" Colin asked.

"You? I've seen you before. What happened to your eye?" the boy asked him.

Colin smiled, trying to be as friendly and unthreatening as possible. "Some asshole punched me," he said. "I got in a fight. It's just swollen. It'll heal."

"Oh," the boy said, giving an unsure smile. "What's your name?"

"Zach."

"Nice to meet you, Zach. I'm Colin. What're you so scared of?"

"I saw something…"

"In one of the rooms? Which one? I'll go with you."

"I'm not sure. One of the ones back there." Zach pointed down the hallway. "There's too many of them."

Colin laughed. "That's for damn sure. Hey, don't worry about it. There are a lot of random people in this house; they're just partygoers that don't know when to leave. That's all. And if you saw something weird, I'm sure it was just your imagination. I've only been working here a couple of days and I've seen some things—mostly when I'm tired. Here, I'll show you the way out."

"You work here?" Zach asked.

Colin shrugged. "I'm painting something for Mr. Klimt."

Zach still looked worried, too worried for a boy his age, Colin thought, but he allowed himself to be led down the hall, toward the back door. "Do you live around here? I can give you a ride home if you'd like?"

"I live in the trailer park just over the tracks. I can walk."

"You sure?"

"Yeah."

"All right." They were at the back door. He opened it. "I'll see you later, Zach."

Zach took a couple of steps to leave, then stopped. He swallowed, clearly unsure if he should say anything. "I was looking for... I was... Have you seen a briefcase anywhere?"

"A briefcase? No. What do you need a briefcase for?"

"It's just..." Total misery fell over Zach's face; the boy's lower lip began to tremble.

Colin dropped to his knees and held the boy. "Hey," he said. "It's okay. It's really okay. Are you in some kind of trouble?"

Zach trembled against him, but didn't say anything.

Colin pulled out the small notepad he kept in his back pocket. "Tell you what," he said (he sounded like his dad when he said things like that). "If you ever need anything, give me a call. Maybe I can help." He scribbled his cell number on a blank page in his notebook and ripped it out. He held it out for the boy to take.

Standing in the doorway, Zach took the note tentatively. The boy turned to leave.

"Ah, hell," Colin said, stopping the boy. "One more thing. I found this in the basement." He held a small card out for the boy to take. "Keep this in your pocket. If you ever see something that you think isn't real, take it out and look at it. Then, if you're dreaming, you'll know it and be able to control it and you won't be afraid. If you're not dreaming, well"—Colin shrugged—"you'll know it's not real; just close your eyes and it'll go away." He smiled.

The boy took the card and scrambled down the path, disappeared around the house.

Colin shook his head. That was weird, he thought. He smiled to himself and closed the door. He needed to get back to work. He was beginning to feel the importance of what he was doing. He was beginning to feel a change coming to his life, a change coming to Mesa Rapids, to his new home.

He'd read about cards like the one he'd given to Zach. That was how he knew what it was used for. By the look on the boy's face, Colin thought, Zach needed it more than he did. Colin knew the difference between dreams and reality. He'd admired the card when he'd found it the night before while exploring the house—trying to find inspiration, a good painting idea, something Klimt would like—old and yellowing paper, in careful calligraphic script: *Is this a dream?*

Chapter 29
LAUREN

The truck jostled and made an alarming thumping sound as Lauren struck the speed bump too fast. She ignored the speedometer, couldn't look at it if she wanted to, her eyes were so bleary. It had been a hallucination brought on by her grief, she knew that, but she could still smell it, thick and coppery, that rotten taste in her mouth.

Now she was taking the long way out of town, along the forest road, out the backside of Mesa Rapids, as if on a day trip to Blue Bear Lake, but when she saw the turnoff for the lake, she planned to keep going, all the way to where the road took her down the other side of the mesa, far away from whatever terrible things were happening in her hometown.

Mark had begged her not to go, had refused to come with her, had refused to believe they were in any danger. Mark had tried to sympathize, had held her and tried to comfort her as best he could, but it hadn't meant anything to Lauren, not when he didn't believe she had reason to be afraid. He'd said it was a terrible tragedy what had happened at her father's ranch, what had happened to her father, but he didn't understand. How could he? The police didn't know what had happened. They said things about fire and wild animals, about spooked horses and disgruntled ranch hands. And they'd asked her strange questions: *Did your father have any enemies? Can you identify the owner of this finger? We're going to show you some pictures and they're pretty graphic. We apologize, but we're trying to understand what the hell happened out there on your father's ranch.*

One of the police officers had told her, when his buddies had left the room, they were still trying to account for the owners of all those severed fingers, why there seemed to be more of them than bodies to match them up with. Lauren had forced herself to keep calm and nodded, her lips pursed so tightly they were white: *What else?* He'd told her it looked as if something had torn through the horses from the inside out. And when she'd asked to see her father's body, they'd refused.

She was out of the neighborhoods now, but still within the bounds of Mesa Rapids, even though it was impossible to see the estate homes through the trees from the road. She kept glancing at the trees, at the green branches as they flashed by. Every time there was a turn in the road, she feared there would be something in her way. She wasn't sure what— a fallen tree would be enough—but what if it was something that had been watching her? Like on her last jog through the park. Something that liked to hide in the foliage and stare? Something that enjoyed the chase?

Ridiculous. Irrational. When she got out of Mesa Rapids and found some place to stop and breathe for a minute, she'd feel better, perhaps even be able to laugh at herself a little.

As she took the next winding turn, she felt her heart quicken—then she breathed a sigh of relief as she saw the next stretch of road was empty. Large cottonwood trees reached their branches over the road, tangled together, creating an arch. The truck bounced beneath the arch and she was immediately severed from most of the sunlight. She flicked on the truck's headlights. She couldn't remember the trees being this big, the ponderosa pines like towers, shivering needles, bark slashed suspiciously in places to reveal pink pulp beneath, and the bulbous cottonwoods, with growths like faces, all of it closing over the road. For a moment, she caught a glimpse of the lake and thought it must be getting late faster than she'd anticipated, the sun going down, filling the clouds with color.

She thought about the radio, but it was broken and she'd never bothered to fix it, so she hummed to herself, but it sounded strange so she stopped. "This is stupid," she said, but immediately regretted it. Her voice betrayed her fear.

The road curved, curved again. She was past the city limits at this point, she was almost sure, although she'd missed the sign. All she had to do was drive through the forest and come out the other side. It was growing stuffy in the truck so she rolled her window down and was surprised by how hot it was outside, and muggy; it was usually cool and crisp this high in the mountains. She took a deep breath and wished for the hundredth time Mark had come with her. She should have waited, been more persistent until she'd convinced him. At the time it had felt important that she leave right away. She no longer cared about her responsibilities; they could wait. She didn't want to be trapped in Mesa Rapids and that's what she felt was going to happen. Her calves were sore, her hips strained, her feet swollen like they'd been stung: something had possessed her that night at Klimt's party to dance and dance for what must have been hours upon hours. That had been the beginning of something.

The truck swung round the curve and Lauren gasped, going rigid in her seat, as the headlights flashed over something large and slow moving in the middle of the road, glinting wetly from the ground, dripping thickly from the trees, reaching toward her.

It was too late to hit the brakes. The thing's mouth twitched into something like a smile, its viscous form a moldering stain. She swerved to the side at the last minute, her skin crawling with loathing. The truck swung, tires screeching on the pavement, turning back the way she'd come.

The truck almost made it all the way around, probably would have if she'd had more time to brake, then thumped at an angle off the side of the road. Lauren felt her head impact with something, heard the loud *knock* in her head. She was jostled in her seat, the strap constricting maddeningly across her body. She saw the tree growing closer at an impossible rate, her feet stomping at nothing, suspended in thin air, unable to find the pedals. The truck ploughed through the underbrush. She pushed on the wheel wildly and the truck slewed at the last minute, striking the tree at an angle.

The crunching sound was deafening. Then—nothing but her ragged breathing. Lauren tried to remain calm. She fumbled with the seat belt, desperate to be free, eventually finding the clasp and ripping it from her shoulders. The glass on her windshield was cracked and her face was inches from the oily bark of the tree through her open side window where the truck had struck it. She was sweating all over her body and her hands were shaking uncontrollably. It was hot, the air thick and hazy. Faintly, she could hear the hissing of escaping steam from beneath the hood of her truck.

Out the windshield, she looked at the road: empty. There was no sign of the thing she'd seen. Of course there wasn't. She knew what she'd seen hadn't been real. The tension was getting to her. She was hallucinating; perhaps she'd drifted off. She needed to breathe. Where was her cell phone? She whipped her head around, looking for where it might have fallen. It was in her pocket. It was stuck deep in the pocket of her jeans. She fumbled across the seats, crawling. Her hand found the latch for the passenger-side door and lifted. The door swung outward. She turned and lowered her feet to the forest floor, where they sank into the topsoil of dead and spongy pine needles.

She leaned against the truck. She forced herself to take deep breaths. She was now able to reach her hand down and remove her cell phone from her pocket. She dialed Mark's number.

He answered on the first ring. "Lauren? Yes? Hello?"

"Mark—"

"Lauren! Thank god! Where are you? You left without saying anything. What happened?"

"I'm on the forest road. I've had an accident. I—"

"What! Are you okay? I'm coming to get you. Are you hurt?"

Lauren could hear Mark grabbing his keys on the other end of the line, slamming things. "I'm okay. I'm not hurt, I just…"

"I'm getting in the car right now. Stay right where you are. On the forest road?"

"Yes. Near the lake." She could hear Mark starting his car. "My phone's going to die."

"All right, then I'll let you go. I'll call you when I'm on the road. Stay right there."

"Okay. Thank y—" but Mark had already hung up.

Lauren slid her phone back into her pocket and sighed. She wasn't sure how far she'd come from town, but she knew it was going to take Mark at least twenty minutes to reach her.

The forest was eerily quiet. There was no breeze, no birds she could see or hear. She hadn't seen a single car on the road since she'd left the city limits. She checked herself in the truck's side-view mirror to be sure she was okay. There was a scratch on her forehead above her left eye, nothing more. She wasn't hurt. She was fine.

Through the trees, she could barely make out a patch of Blue Bear Lake. She wiped sweat from her forehead and walked a little ways between the trees. The lake was dark. She walked up a small hill and looked out through the forest. Her heart kicked chokingly in her throat and she could feel the alkaline dump of adrenaline once more filling her veins. From where she stood, through an opening in the trees, what she saw was the same thing she'd seen earlier, when she'd turned the truck around and decided to take the road across the mesa, when she'd reached the edge of the hill and found herself looking over the valley, what she'd seen filling it.

The lake was thick, rippled in lazy threads. Its beaches frothed, sands licked dark with crimson. The sky reflected its color: red as a deepening sunset. Its waters were blood, swampy, a sea. And the air hung with the rancidity of it, heavy and warm, stinging her nose, leaving a metallic taste in her mouth. She could see where the forest came to an abrupt conclusion, where the road would be severed, and the sea of blood began, unending as far as her eyes could perceive to the horizon line.

Lauren turned and ran down the hill, back to her truck, forced her way in through the passenger door until she was sitting in the driver's seat once again. She didn't care if there was something wrong with the truck. She couldn't wait for Mark. She forced the key and the starter turned, rumbled, the engine ground to life. She reversed around the tree, screeching wood on metal, and backed onto the road. She pointed the truck back the way she'd come, back toward Mesa Rapids, and began to drive as fast as she dared along the winding road.

It wasn't long before she realized the roads had changed, and she no longer had any idea where or in which direction she was going.

PART TWO

COLIN'S JOURNAL

"I don't paint dreams or nightmares, I paint my own reality."

—Frida Kahlo

CHAPTER 30

*I*remember that first week with my new job, after smugly paying my rent in cash to Jeremy, staying up nights in my room looking out the window watching Klimt's mansion. I already wasn't sleeping well and I was nervous about what I was supposed to be doing. I had some ideas, some roughly sketched designs in this notebook that I'd shown to Klimt, which had received noncommittal nods of approval, but I had no idea what he really wanted from me. I was still wondering why he hired me and for what purpose. I hung out with Maddie a little when Jeremy wasn't around, but we never talked about anything serious. I don't think either one of us knew what to say.

On my first day, I took my sketchbook and a pen into a seemingly quiet corner of the Upshaw Mansion to hash out some ideas. I hadn't been in there for ten minutes when a man in a ruffled tuxedo staggered across the hall and onto the bench before the grand piano and began to play something banging and dramatic in a sloppy sort of way. I tried to ignore him, but when he paused and said to me, "Wagner," I had to respond and nodded, "Uh-huh." The man then said, in a perfectly crisp English accent, "I was with the band." He was referring to the party of the night before. I stood and walked out of the room.

I had the hardest time concentrating. Whenever I found a seemingly quiet place to brainstorm, there was always someone around to distract me, women with wrinkled dresses and hairstyles flattened from spending the night over, men with their ties loosened and thrown over their shoulders, always drunk, sometimes laughing. It was as if they followed me, found something to admire in each room I visited— mumbling in groups over a particular painting, then shuffling to the couches to lounge and smile. I had to keep moving. I found the library, where I'd been with Maddie at the party we'd crashed, and thought it was empty, closing the door behind me, sinking gratefully into one of the chairs. But before I could even get my notebook out, the middle-aged man with bottle-cap glasses appeared from behind a shelf of books and said, "The hum? Do you hear the hum?" I asked him what he was doing there and he said he was hiding from his wife, trying to sober up before he saw her again. "Still?" I asked him, since it had been several days since the party, but he only shook his head and told me he'd been all over the house. I stood, shrugged and left.

What a strange place.

Chapter 31

Several days go by sometimes and I sleep on a couch in a corner, or in the small bedroom at the end of the hall, or slouched in a chair in the basement. I feel close to discovery so I don't want to leave, don't want to return home, to have to deal with my roommates, especially Jeremy—whom, I suspect, hates me now. But still, no matter what I do, I can't get Maddie out of my head—she's all I want.

Sometimes, when my brain feels like soggy oat bran and I simply can't concentrate anymore, and the music from above begins to feel like a pulsing headache, I go for walks in the middle of the night. I have discovered, if I cut through the yard on the side of the house, there is a narrow street, just before the field opens to the train tracks, lined by dark houses with a small dive bar nestled among them called Elephant House. Inside, the place is dark and smoky. There is an old jukebox in the corner. The bartender is an aging hippie with long, scrappy white hair and a face deeply lined from a lifetime of drinking, with a throaty voice that's difficult to understand.

My first time there, only one other patron sat at the bar. He was older than me, still a young man, but with one of those dark and pointy faces always in need of a shave. I ordered a beer and nearly emptied the bottle in a single drink. "Thirsty, eh?" the man said to me. I said I was and he offered to buy me another. We talked for what felt like hours. The man's name was Donnie and I shook his hand and told him I was Colin and he said he'd been coming to Elephant House for as long as he could remember. He told me the bar wasn't well-known by the locals, that it was a well-kept neighborhood secret and that a lot of things happened there that some folks in town would find offensive. When I asked him what those kinds of things might be, he looked me closely in the eyes. When I looked him right back, which was easy considering how much I'd had to drink at this point, he smiled, shook his head dismissively. "It's a good place to pick up girls," he said. "Sometimes it gets crazy in here. But most times," Donnie said, waving his hand at the empty bar, "it's like this."

The second time I went to Elephant House, it was a little busier. There were several men slumped over the bar and a pair of feminine figures sat at a table in a shadowy corner. The only sounds in the place were mumbling voices and scraping chairs. I took an open stool at the bar and ordered a beer from the grumbling bartender. It took my eyes a moment to adjust to the dimness, since most of the lights above the bar had burned out, before I realized Donnie was sitting right next to me, turned and grinning with all his teeth, waiting for me to notice him. He slapped me on the back and said it was good to see me. I told him the same. We talked for a while, about nothing in particular, drinking beer after beer, until eventually Donnie said one of the girls from the corner had been eyeing me. I turned to look, but even with my eyes adjusted I still couldn't see either of the women's faces. He told me he had to go anyway and why don't I go over and introduce myself. Donnie dropped more than enough money on the counter to pay for both our drinks and stood. For a moment he swayed and I reached out to help him, but he insisted he was all right. I watched him walk toward the door, clumping awkwardly in his black leather boots as if they didn't fit right, one of them turned strangely to the side as if his foot was broken. "Can't walk in these things," he whispered, then pushed open the door and disappeared into the smoky night.

Now I don't have much experience with bars, but you always hear about meeting women in such places. I don't know why I did it. I didn't think about it; it felt almost like I didn't have a choice. I walked over and asked the women if I could join them. I remember my heart was pounding, but it seems so easy now. One of the women said, "Sure," and the other nodded. I bought them both drinks and we talked for a long time. It's funny, I can't remember their names now—I was very drunk—and I can't see their faces in my head either; I only know one of them had darker hair than the other, and when the darker-haired one had excused herself to go to the bathroom, the dark-haired one had turned to me and asked if I'd like to get out of there.

I chickened out. I wanted to—at least part of me did— but it didn't feel right. I knew what she meant by "get out of there," but I hardly knew her. I can't even remember her name now. I wish I could. It's strange when you start a new life in a new place—you feel like you can do anything. It feels like an opportunity to start fresh and change how people see you, to change who you are, but it's never quite that simple, is it?

CHAPTER 32

I've finally started something. It's not something I'd usually try, and I'm not sure it's what Klimt is looking for, but a part of me feels it is the right thing to do.

I've discovered a room on the side of the house at the end of a long hallway that looks out on the street outside. From the window, from between the overgrown trees, I can see my house and sometimes my roommates smoking on the porch. When they come outside, I like to stop everything I'm doing and watch them. I want to join them, but I know I can't. I have work to do.

In this room I've started constructing an intricate sculpture. I've scavenged all sorts of random things from the house, bits of old furniture and things from the kitchen, as well as my tools: chisels, scrappers, a hacksaw, and paints, in squashed tubes like lizards crushed in the road. I have a blowtorch, along with a number of small canisters of gas, and have even used a couple of the empty tanks in my sculpture.

Already my sculpture is getting large, taking on a vaguely humanoid shape. I may need to scavenge more materials soon. It is a twisted hulk, made from wood and scraps of metal. It is held together mostly by screws and bolts, but also nails and glue. At its base is a large metal cage I found in one of the rooms, its wire bars that I have meticulously cut and bent into flowing shapes, ribbons and spirals. Above that, there is a wheel from a bicycle, turned at an angle, which still spins, and gears and blades and drills from some old power tools I found in the basement. And above that, pieces from a chair I shattered, one of its legs turned out and one of the empty gas canisters fused to its end like a boxing glove.

The top of my sculpture is still a work in progress, jagged and disarranged, and still needs a lot of work, but the center of my piece is nearly complete. I've stretched and bent wires from various parts to surround a chunk of wood I spent days carving into a swirling abstract shape. I call this shaped piece of wood "the bird," although I'm not sure why. It certainly doesn't look like a bird. It more closely resembles a heart, the wires coming off it like veins, tangled over and around my sculpture's other protuberances.

Sometimes, out of the corner of my eye, I see the bird shift a little, pulse, the wires swaying, but when I turn to look full upon it, all is still.

This feels important, what I'm doing. My sculpture feels important. Klimt told me to do what felt right and that's exactly what I'm doing, but I hope he doesn't find me in this room for a few days. I don't want him to see what I'm working on. I'm worried he won't like it. I need this job.

CHAPTER 33

I'm not sure if this was a dream...

I fell asleep in the room with my sculpture the other day and woke up in the middle of the night with my entire body shaking. I was terrified. I had to get out of the Upshaw Mansion, desperately and immediately. I groped to my feet and forced the window open. I pushed myself through the opening and nearly fell headfirst into the bushes outside.

I stood and it was strange. The ground rippled as if it were a viscous sludge. The sky was dark and close. I was afraid if I reached up, I might be able to dip my hand into it.

I limped away toward my own house, where my roommates, my friends—where Maddie lived and waited for me. I tripped and could feel the earth vibrating beneath me. It didn't feel solid, as if I might begin to sink into it.

I was tired, weak. I lifted myself and turned to look back at the Upshaw Mansion. It was massive, crawling into the soupy night sky. Everything around it bent and swayed—the trees, the mists—but it remained solid, real; even its windows, like gaping black holes, were still.

Then something drew my attention. I looked at the bushes I'd fallen into below the window. Something was coming up from the ground. It wriggled, gasped, had a shifting form, like shadow. It freed itself and I watched it stalk away into the dark, moving around to the front of the mansion.

I picked myself up and walked back to the cluster of bushes. I was no longer afraid, only numb, somehow excited. There was a dark puddle *where the form had come up. I dropped to my knees, reached my hand out. My fingers came back, sticky and dark. I staggered away.*

When I reached a large tree, I collapsed against it. I no longer had the strength to lift myself. I watched the night, trees and sky and ground all bending into each other, all in one place, in one time.

In the morning, I was back in the room with my sculpture. There was blood on my fingers, probably from the night before, when I must have cut them on my sculpture.

CHAPTER 34

When I woke up this morning, I found I'd destroyed my sculpture. I must have done it. I'm the only one here. I've been tired, sometimes drifting off in the middle of my work. It's okay. It had to be done. I need to find something else to do, something better.

Klimt hated my sculpture. When he saw it, he laughed. He called it "modern-art trash." I didn't know what to say. I wanted to defend my work, to tell him I was only doing what I was compelled to do, what he asked me to do, but he only shook his head, "No, Colin. You can do better."

So now I'm back where I started, sitting on the floor in the center of the room, staring at the wreckage. It's as if an explosion has gone off in the room. Bits and pieces of my sculpture flung to every corner: fractured scraps of wood, tangled balls of wire, an unrecognizable mass stomped to a crumpled heap.

Among the tangled wire, I found the bird, still intact. I untwisted the wires, one at a time, pulling them out of each other, until I was able to free the bird.

I need to figure out what Klimt wants. He's the one paying me, after all. He's the one who is allowing me to be a "professional artist." That's what I've always wanted.

Isn't it?

CHAPTER 35

*I*finally went back to the house and hung out with my roommates. I had a good time. They all pretended like I hadn't been gone, even Maddie, who kept giving me nervous smiles and averting her eyes when I caught her looking at me. We didn't talk, not really. I wanted to, but I didn't know what to say. It's too late, I think. It's weird.

I've reassembled most of my sculpture in my room at the house. I figured just because Klimt didn't like it, that doesn't mean I should destroy it. It's come together a little differently this time, more gears and blades and gas canisters, and is now centered about the bird at its heart. But I've been hurried. I need to get back to the Upshaw Mansion and continue my work for Klimt. I know he wouldn't like it if he knew I'd wasted several days putting my own sculpture back together, but fuck him. It feels good to have some time off away from the Upshaw Mansion.

Earlier today, Jeremy came into my room and got a good look at my sculpture. I could tell he'd been drinking and wanted to give me a hard time about things, but when he saw the sculpture, he seemed taken aback. He froze. "My god," he said. "It…it looks like you!"

I laughed. What else could I do?

CHAPTER 36

I'm back at the Upshaw Mansion. I haven't gone back home to the house in a week. I have too much work to do. I've made progress and Klimt is pleased. I should have known right away I was meant to work in the basement. It is the only place in the house I am able to be without being disturbed. The rest of the house is always buzzing with people. The basement feels right. I even began a treatment on one of the concrete walls, afraid when Klimt came to check on me he'd be angry, but he only smiled, pleased with what I'd done, encouraging me to "pursue what feels natural" and then left me to continue.

These past few nights I've gone out—because I haven't been sleeping well and when I do drift off I dream and I don't like to dream; the nightmares are too vivid—around through the alley at the back of the mansion, down that strangely quiet street to Elephant House. I haven't seen Donnie there all week, but I have picked up some women— weird, lost women—which I'm not proud of. It's strange. When I'm at Elephant House, I don't feel like myself. Elephant House is my escape; I forget myself and don't think about my actions.

The first woman I picked up was Sabrina. One of her ears was melted into a healed flat patch of shiny skin from when her stepfather had put her head to the stove when she was a little girl, she told me reluctantly. And she had scars up and down her arms from when she used to cut herself as a teenager. She turned the lights off in the bedroom back at her place as she undressed, while I waited in bed. We talked after and it was pleasant and I turned on the bedside lamp so I could watch her lips move while she spoke and the second time the light didn't matter and I watched the gleam on her ear and on her little white teeth as she came on top of me. She was cute and gentle and I was sad when she told me she was leaving the country in the morning and I never saw her again.

Melissa was another. She had one of those aggressive jet-black haircuts with bangs that cut a straight line right above her severe eyes. Her dark red lips pursed as she pushed me down on the backseat of her convertible. When she ripped off my shirt, I heard some of the buttons scatter over the hood and to the street. Then her own top was off and she wasn't wearing a bra and her nipples were pierced and so was her tongue and she tore the belt out of my pants, threw it like a snake undeserving of her attention, and immediately put my dick in her mouth. Then she was on top of me in only her black knee-high boots and piercings and all I could do was lay there and let her do her thing. When she was done, she pushed me from her car, threw my clothes on the street, and, without bothering to put on her own clothes, floored her car with a screech down the street and out of sight without giving me a second glance. I put my clothes back on in the dark and slunk back to Klimt's house and finished myself into a tissue in the basement.

Then there was Carrie. She used to be a Playboy centerfold she told me, even though right away I thought she looked too bony and flat-chested for that sort of thing. She said she'd retired from that life; too much pressure. After we left the dimness of the bar, I could see the crow's feet around her eyes. She was a little older than I'd thought, but I didn't care. She liked to party, she said, and fueled on numerous Cape Cods and a couple tabs of ecstasy each, we thrummed out of Elephant House and down the street to her place, where she put rock 'n' roll music on loud enough to wake the neighborhood and we danced on the warm wave of the present and then fucked in every position we could think of, mostly her ideas, and then, as the morning began to creep into the sky, passed out exhausted on her bed. That midafternoon, as we awoke slowly, she turned her mascara-smeared face to me and said, "I love you," although admitted she couldn't remember my name.

We spent the next day together. She made us breakfast—scrambled eggs and toast with jam—and I ate quietly at the table while she talked about her life in the "industry" and about her ex-husband, some sort of *porn producer. She kept pausing, saying, "I love you," and then quickly talking about something else before I was forced to say it back. By the time the sun began to set, she was crying and telling me about her rape. When I went to her and tried to comfort her, she pushed me away, violently, and then began to yell at me, saying I'd taken advantage of her, saying I was just like all the other men; what made me any different? "Well, say something!" she said. And when I stood there with my mouth open, in a dumbfounded shock, completely at a loss for words, she pushed me and I fell to the ground, clattering dishes and the jar of jam from the table to spatter over the floor. "Say something!" I watched her snatch a knife from the wooden block sitting on the kitchen counter. "Say something!" And I ran out the door, slamming it behind me.*

Sometimes I wonder: can a woman like that ever heal from the hurt of her past? Can any of us? I think about that canted smile of hers, of her bony curve-less figure— like fucking a skeleton—and her bright gray eyes trapped in a face ten years older than it should be. If I had said "I love you" back, would things have been different? How can the right words at the right moments change things?

I waited a couple of days and then tried to go back one night after a few drinks at Elephant House. I knocked on the door, but there were no lights shining inside. I walked around to the side of the house and peered through one of the windows with the shades undrawn. The house was empty, the furniture gone. A broom sat forlornly propped against the fireplace mantel. A single can of paint. She was gone. I wandered back out to the street. None of the streetlights worked and it was very dark, and quiet. On impulse, I checked her mailbox. Inside there was a curled piece of yellowing paper:

    Colin,
    I'm sorry. Maybe I'll see you in the next life. Please forgive me.
    —Carrie

And that was it. She was gone. And when I was done reading her note and looked up, I was suddenly aware of how utterly quiet it was on the street—creepy quiet. I began walking back the way I'd come. There were no lights, not a single glowing house window, and only the moonlight to show me where I was going. So quiet: no insects, only the scrape of my tennis shoes on the sidewalk, even my labored breathing audible in the night. I had to stop, hold my breath, and listen, to be sure I wasn't being followed, that it was only the echo of my own footsteps, coming back to me from that cavernous street, chasing me away.

It's laughable really, that I should feel so afraid. In the moment, when I'm doing things, it feels like all fun and games, the alcohol erasing all the consequences, sex the only motive that matters. It isn't until later the bandages are peeled back and the wounds found to be infected. A deep loneliness. A longing sadness. There's so little that matters. Always hiding from something. I want to go back, speak with Maddie, make things right, but I don't. I'm too chickenshit. She deserves better than me. That's the true fear.

CHAPTER 37

L ast night, I had another nightmare.

It was terrifying. It is difficult to explain the immensity of my fear, of the looming dread I felt after. It was odd, as if I might still be sleeping. As if I might never be fully awake.

In the dream I am at a party, in the mansion, and everyone is grinning. We are all dancing in circles, in the main ballroom. But it is dark, and something is coming; everyone can feel its approaching strides. We've woken something, but there is nowhere we can go; all we can do is circle and spin, circle and spin. And slowly, I come to the cold realization that the shadows have played a trick on me, and not a single smile is real, that everyone wears an equal grimace of despair. And something is coming. It is massive, whatever it is, and I don't want to see it, but I know I will. It is written in the dream-script. And that is when the mouths of all the people around me drop open and the screams fill the air and the house begins to distort and grow out of all proportions, concave and convex angles splitting open into impossibilities I am unable to fully perceive, people's faces melting and stretching, and the stairs somehow climbing upward while at the same time plunging into the abyss beneath my feet...

CHAPTER 38

Sometimes I'll open a door and see something crazy. I saw a little girl stacking empty beer bottles all the way to the ceiling once and when she noticed me she put her finger to her mouth to signal I should be quiet and I closed the door. I saw a puddle of blood at the foot of a bed, but when I blinked, it was gone. I saw a man wearing some sort of furry animal costume and one of those plain white-plastic masks having sex doggy-style with a woman wearing fairy wings. It's a strange house. I don't know sometimes if I'm hallucinating or really seeing some of this stuff. It's like I said: I haven't been sleeping well. Okay, actually, I haven't been sleeping at all really. Everything feels surreal when you're tired enough.

When I was a kid, I used to have these sleepovers with my friend Ben where we'd stay up late all night playing video games and not get any sleep. We'd go nonstop from the moment we got out of school, through the night, until light began to filter through the blinds on the windows we'd not bothered to close. By morning, our fingers would be sore and our eyes bleary and we no longer cared how well we did in the games or who won and who lost. We'd laugh at the stupidest stuff, rolling absurdly around on the floor.

My mom used to read stories to me at night. Even when I was old enough to read for myself, she'd still read to me every night. Books like James and the Giant Peach and The Tale of Peter Rabbit. Then later, things like The Chronicles of Narnia and The Lord of the Rings books. Once she read me Treasure Island because I begged her to. I used to watch her lips moving, or her large brown eyes tracking the words. I could hear it in her voice when she got to the exciting parts, as she began to read faster and faster, and I loved that she enjoyed the stories as much as I did. Then she'd reach the end of a chapter and her eyes would turn down to me and I'd say "Please, Mom! Please! One more!" And then she'd flip through the pages to see how long the next section was and sometimes she'd read another chapter and sometimes she'd insist I go to sleep. Sometimes there were visible bruises on my mom's face. Sometimes I didn't sleep even after she turned out the lights.

There were days as a kid when I was so tired I'd see things. Usually just blurs of movement at the corner of my eye, or mistake a boulder among some bushes in someone's yard for a crouching person. But occasionally I'd see something like a group of kids distantly in the park, circling something, kicking at it, and when they noticed me, they'd all look up at me with identical hate-filled faces and I'd run all the rest of the way home.

Did I mention I saw Donnie again? He was at Elephant House and we talked for a long while. I told him about my one-night stands and he clapped me on the back and grinned, ordered another round. I've told him about my project, about getting paid to paint for some rich guy, and he said he might be able to help me, but only when I was ready. He said, "I'm your friend." I told him I'd let him know.

I'm still working in the basement. It is large and spacious—a single room nearly the size of an entire floor of the house with concrete walls and a concrete floor. Everywhere boxes are piled nearly to the exposed pipes, which rattle and tap constantly. The piles create corridors with open areas like individual rooms. I've settled into an area near the bottom of the stairs, laying out my paints and brushes on a table made from a piece of plywood laid over some boxes. I haven't explored the entire basement—there's so much junk down here and very little light. I've finally found a place where no one bothers me as I try to figure out what the hell I'm going to do to assure Klimt continues to pay me. Considering the money I'm making, I'll do whatever it takes.

Sometimes, when I grow tired of painting, I'll explore my new studio a little, looking through the stacks of yellowing documents, strange unrecognizable tools, and aging garments that look, to me, like costumes. I pull the cord under the rickety wooden stairs that lead up into the house, and the swinging, uncovered lightbulb casts a sickly glow over the stacks of boxes slumped against the cold concrete walls. Sitting in a rickety chair I found by the slashed Ping-Pong table, I slide one of the boxes free and begin to leaf through its ancient contents.

What began as curiosity, and boredom (and lack of artistic inspiration), has now, somehow, become as important as the work itself, as I begin to see patterns, to find things so unusual they are like pieces in a puzzle, evidence of transgressions hidden from human history. I've become absorbed, forgetting where I am and what I'm supposed to be doing, and time passes, forgotten, around me. I must look crazy, sitting there surrounded by my own little stacks and piles, breathing in shallow gasps, hair hanging in my face, licking my lips feverishly. I've found some odd things tucked in among the stacks of musty newspapers and sales receipts. Creepy things. A lock of blonde hair taped to a plain cardboard sheet—"Daddy's little girl" scrawled shakily beneath the straggling strands. A wooden box carved with some sort of animal with a long body and tiny pointed teeth, a single yellowed molar rattling around inside. A balled-up T-shirt stained with blood. A page ripped from a book with colored illustrations of insects. A small card with the words "Is This A Dream?" written on it with a calligraphy quill. A crumpled piece of stationery, still fragrant with perfume, a note begun but never finished: "Dear Mom, The doctors say I may be able to come home soon. They say the air here is doing me some good, but sometimes I wonder. At night I hear things, people talking about me, discussing whether I'm going to live or die. Isn't that strange? The other day I thought I saw—" That was all. The note was dated September 14, 1944. I found a wooden, handmade Advent calendar with little drawers to open for each day in December before Christmas. My grandmother used to get me the ones you can buy at the store made out of cardboard with the chocolates inside when I was a kid. Each compartment on the wooden one I found was stuffed with a different kind of animal hair, red like a fox's, or brown and coarse like a bear's. And I found some words scrawled on the back of a handwritten bill of sale for three dozen eggs and a bottle of bleach in thick pencil: "I'm *here/Can you hear me?/Please don't go/The gnomes on the wallpaper are jeering again/He moves under the floorboards." The bill of sale was from "Joe's Market," undated and unsigned. It feels to me like all these things are somehow connected. It feels like if I look hard enough, I'll discover their secret. I know it sounds crazy—it's just a bunch of old junk in a basement. But there's something here, something beneath the surface. And so I keep exploring the basement, looking through boxes, hoping to find inspiration, a clue to Klimt's intentions, something about the past owners of this house, and where all this might have come from.*

Hang on. I have to go. Klimt is here to discuss my progress…

PART THREE
MESA RAPIDS

"This is a valley of ashes—a fantastic farm where ashes grow like wheat into ridges and hills and grotesque gardens; where ashes take the forms of houses and chimneys and rising smoke and, finally, with a transcendent effort, of men who move dimly and already crumbling through the powdery air."

—F. Scott Fitzgerald, *The Great Gatsby*

CHAPTER 39
REVEREND TRUMBULL

The original name given to Aspen Mesa and the surrounding lands by the Ute people, who lived and hunted its forests before white settlers began to colonize them, is now forgotten. The white people came out of the east and by the 1880s there were several families of farmers and ranchers established in the area. Unlike most other areas of the western United States, the native peoples gave little resistance to the colonists—their chief at the time, and his reportedly lovely wife, readily forsaking the lands in favor of the reservations established for their people farther north. The settlers called their village "Mesa Town" and quickly prospered as their crops and orchards flourished and their cattle grew plump.

Unlike many of the surrounding areas, gold was never discovered in Mesa Rapids, although significant amounts of silver were collected from the nearby mountains until the mine dried up by the turn of the century. By the mid-twentieth century, uranium was being mined from the nearby mountains, coring tunnels still farther into the depths of the earth. By the 1970s, oil shale development became prominent in the valley below the mesa, digging, recovering shale—known as the "Rock That Burns"—and processing it to produce oil. By the 1980s and '90s, much of the valley below the mesa was stripped and polluted, waste from the mines running off into the river, fields left fallow as their soils became less fertile, alkaline and over-seeded. Only the grounds atop the mesa were preserved, mostly by wealthy landowners, horse ranchers and resort homeowners. The settlers and citizens of what was officially named Mesa Rapids in the 1920s built over and dug into the land, lost respect for it. The Utes could have told them something of the importance of keeping a connection with the land, especially in such a place, where the shamans were said to communicate with the voices of the dead in the form of a pervasive hum.

During the early years of the town, most of its citizens were considered Christian, but few were practicing—this being the Wild West after all, most having little time for rituals and distraction from their hardworking farmer's lives.

Until one day when a man by the name of Gillian Trumbull rode into town. He came alone, bringing with him a small wagon driven by a single pony like the ones the Ute people were known for breeding. With him he also brought a puritanical religious zeal and charisma like no one in those parts had ever seen. Within a week, he had more than half the town rallied together in someone's barn, a cross of branches thatched together upon its roof. With a fiery passion, Reverend Trumbull declared Mesa Town a sacred place, "which I hereby decree be called Mesa Rapids," although no one was ever sure exactly where the name came from, the white water of the meandering river not being the most impressive sight around. "I will show this town the *true* way of the Lord. I will show you all the *true* path to enlightenment. Together we will forge a *true* pathway to the heavenly afterlife!"

Within a month, citizens were volunteering their time to erect a church, built from limestone bricks quarried and carved from the earth. People spent their mornings as farmers and their afternoons as stonemasons, shaping rock and mixing mortar. In the evenings, they prayed together, supplications to a god few of them understood, but whom Reverend Trumbull assured them would reward them their just deserves.

Within the church, statues of faceless men and women were placed along the handmade wooden pews. Anyone with artistic ability was given a brush and some paints and assigned a section of the wall on which to embellish images of their choosing; they were told to open their hearts to the Lord and paint whatever moved them. Some painted trees and some painted mountains.

Some painted nameless people and some painted their fathers and mothers and some painted interpretations of Jesus Christ. Some painted suns and others moons. Some painted scenes of beasts from legend—satyrs, and centaurs, and griffins—while others painted creatures of their own invention, with long arms and large teeth, with purple skin and drooping eyes, with hairy bodies and human hands for feet.

The church, when finished, was wonderfully colorful, and a delight to the townsfolk. Near the front an ornate chair was positioned—shaped painstakingly by the young Bradley Upshaw, who made his living as the town carpenter and furniture shop owner—on the raised podium. Decreed as the chair of God, it was forbidden to all, even to Revered Trumbull himself, reserved exclusively for the divine presence of the Lord. Some claimed to see a corporeal form, barely visible, during the heated shouts of hallelujah during the reverend's exclamations of holy hellfire from the pulpit. Most, however, never saw such things and appreciated the chair for its symbolic value alone.

Within months, almost everyone in town was swayed to this new religion. Every night they prayed for the forgiveness of their sins and for the unrighteous to be smote down by the Lord. Sexual congress of any sort outside the privacy of the marital bed was strictly forbidden. The doors to the local saloon were shut and the imbibing of intoxicating liquids was banned. When Dell Overmyer, known for his horse-breeding abilities, was discovered with Cathleen Renner in the barn by one of his ranch hands, he immediately accused the young Cathleen of witchcraft and she was hanged from a cross on the outskirts of town—left with her throat cut, for the birds, and, eventually, the coyotes. When a man and his wife and daughter came through town in a covered wagon on their way to California seeking supplies, they were called *outsiders* and told to keep going, but when the man demanded to at least have a drink before moving on, pounding on the locked doors and windows to the closed saloon (which had been converted into "Joe's Market"), he had been shot dead in the dusty street. Later, in the middle night, the man's wife wailing and crying over the dead body of her husband in the street, someone had shot her as well just to shut her up. The man and woman's three-year-old was coaxed out of the wagon the next morning and was taken in and raised by the Clemens family. When she was old enough, Rachel Clemens married Nathaniel Upshaw, and eventually became part of an important and influential family in the history of Mesa Rapids.

There were those in town, however, who, despite the feelings of the majority, refused to attend the Holy Rapids Church of the Lord. One of these individuals was Joseph Keller, who, for a time, owned a small bookshop in town. He and his wife Chloe—a well-read and learned woman—after closing the bookshop for lack of patronage, the followers of Reverend Trumbull having little use for literature other than that given them by their new leader, kept their three boys and themselves in their small cabin with their modest apple orchard and garden, and tried to stay out of the affairs of the townsfolk. But as the months went by, pressures from the townsfolk intensified and it became more and more difficult for the Kellers to continue to live and do business with people that were increasingly unfriendly and sometimes hostile to them. Joseph and Chloe began to make arrangements to take their chances and head west.

Their three boys—Adam, Jeffrey, and George—were excited about the move, having seen a picture in a newspaper that showed the rich wonders of the west, and couldn't help but share their exciting plans with their friends at the one-room schoolhouse in town. Only days before they were to finally leave, in the middle of a sweltering summer in which the crops were less verdant than the previous few years due to lack of rain, a large crowd of "Rapidians" lined up at the front of the Kellers' house, torches and rifles held aloft, faces obscured in shadow. The mob demanded the three boys be left behind, that they be raised under the teachings of the church. When Joseph and Chloe attempted to sneak their children out the back of the house, they were chased into the trees. Chloe, being a better shot than her husband, with the only rifle they owned, took up a spot between two trees, her foot propped up on a small boulder, and managed to gun down four of the mob members before she took a bullet in the throat, while Joseph fled with their children deep into the woods. But the mob was relentless, and when they caught up to Joseph, who stood resolutely between the mob and his children, they cut him down where he stood. The mob found two of the children, who were hauled back to town and hanged from crosses to starve slowly for the transgressions of their parents. The Keller house was burned. Jeffrey was never found.

When Greg Mason was found to have killed his entire family with a claw hammer and then turned the hammer on himself, his body slumped in a rocking chair, his face completely destroyed, it was discovered he'd been distilling his own whiskey and there were signs he'd been bottling large portions of it, indicating there were others involved. "It is clear Mr. Mason was in league with the devil," Reverend Trumbull said at his next sermon. "He has paid for his transgressions. Justice has been served—the Lord's justice! He will burn for eternity in the hellfire beneath us!" A search was conducted, from house to house, led by the reverend himself, and others were discovered with hidden reserves of alcohol and other illicit materials, including items traded or collected from the Ute people—a beaded belt depicting a herd of elk, a ceremonial drum, pottery and arrowheads. A man who refused to give up his carved figurine of a naked woman was hanged. Things were taken and destroyed and houses were burned and people were crucified: "Smote down by the Lord!" Haley Klein, who had been left a widow taking care of her four children all on her own after her husband had taken sick with fever the previous summer, saw and talked with her husband at the edge of the woods while gathering berries from the rustling raspberry bushes. When she got home, she shot her four children and then shot herself through the head. Samuel Hillman ran into town screaming for the reverend after the tilled cuts left by his plow in his fields began to well up with blood. Peter Gregory watched the scarecrow, terrified from the window out the front of his house, walking around in the middle of the night, sometimes stopping to look up at the moon and grin. After a couple of young Ute men rode into town looking to trade goods with the people of Mesa Rapids and were castrated and left to bleed to death in the streets, the fire of 1857, which spread through town burning more than half of it to the ground before it finally died out, was blamed on the evil brought to the land by the Ute people.

The church, left miraculously untouched—divinely so, some claimed—by the fire, became a refuge for those whose homes had been lost while they began to rebuild. In the coming months, Reverend Trumbull's preaching became increasingly passionate, involving much pounding of his fists on the pulpit and screaming of the devil among them. The reverend claimed he was going to confront the evil that had come to Mesa Rapids, stand up to the devil, and exorcise the insidious presence from their homes and lands. He said his purity of heart and his embracing the love of Jesus Christ would protect him. He prepared, bleaching his robes white and wearing a crown made from twisted branches. Every morning, he was brought fresh roses to fix about his robes, the shriveled ones from the days before left to dry collected in a great brass holy bowl. The day before his confrontation, which was to begin as soon as the sun began to set, Reverend Trumbull gave a powerful and moving benediction, his words of such conviction they moved the entire town, words of such power the ground itself is said to have trembled, the sunlight brightened, the blossoms bloomed. But the reverend's words were never recorded, and so history is left to interpret Reverend Trumbull's intentions as it will.

The next morning, the reverend was found dismembered. Parts of him were discovered scattered to opposite sides of town. A foot was found floating in the horse trough by the Oldtown Restaurant and Inn (formerly Joe's Market). A handless arm segment was stuffed in a mailbox, the missing hand found resting atop a roof several houses down the street. Various internal bits were found to have been made into a feast by Farmer Jackson's pigs.

At least, according to the journals of Harold Upshaw, who claims to have been an unwilling participant and silent observer during those sordid times, these things are said to have happened. The history books record only a day known as "Black Sunday," on which the hardships of the town, brought on by the hot summer and failing crops due to the drought, came to a dramatic conclusion involving a restless mob and resulting in the killing of Reverend Trumbull. After that, the church was destroyed and things are said to have returned to normal.

Harold Upshaw died without sharing his journal with a single soul, and when his wife Ethel, under a loose floorboard, later discovered it, Ethel could only shake her head and wonder at the length in which her husband had hidden his unwell mind from her, their children, and the citizens of Mesa Rapids.

Chapter 40
THE UPSHAWS

Harold and Ethel's children soon became productive and even prestigious members of Mesa Rapids society, including Nathaniel, who, after his mother's death, took over the family farm, married Rachel Clemens, and discovered a huge deposit of oil shale on his property while his wife was pregnant with their first child. At the turn of the twentieth century, oil shale production was popular for lighting and heating, but soon the demand for oil of any sort grew, as did the popularity of the automobile. Nathaniel and his family became rich, and the Upshaw Mansion was built.

Nathaniel and Rachel had four daughters and one son, Charles, the youngest. Rachel died during childbirth and Nathaniel mourned her loss deeply. Their daughters, all of them with strikingly beautiful dark hair and light eyes, married various businessmen, to whom they were introduced through their father's connections. Each of them, in turn, took the opportunity to escape their tiny hometown, moved to various cities with their husbands, and so, at least according to the historians, passed into obscurity.

The Upshaws' only son Charles, however, chose to stay in Mesa Rapids, taking over the family business when he was old enough. He married Darlene Harris, a no-nonsense woman who ran a tight house, directing the servants while she raised their seven daughters. And under Darlene's leadership, the Upshaw house thrived, while under Charles's leadership, business continued to prosper.

For many years, the Upshaws enjoyed their success. The mansion was expanded, built larger and larger as their wealth grew, although what they could possibly do with all of those rooms was a wonder to the citizens of Mesa Rapids.

As Charles grew into middle age and his father, Nathaniel, became an old man, he became less and less social. He left the dealings of the business to others and sequestered himself in his home. His wife reported he spent his days in the library with his books, pouring over old texts, looking for something. Darlene was not afraid to tell folks in the town market she thought whatever her husband was looking for, she felt he was not likely to find, although she continued to dutifully frequent the library for him, to pick up the books he required. It was soon common knowledge among the townsfolk that Mr. Charles Upshaw had likely lost his mind.

Charles was not seen for months, leaving his mansion only long enough to attend his father's funeral, even then refusing to speak with anyone. His father had been found along a path in the woods where Nathaniel had often walked, still, on his back, his lifeless eyes staring open at the sky. In Nathaniel's hand, a crumpled letter was found, written seemingly from Rachel, his long-dead wife. The letter said how much she missed Nathaniel's embrace and that he'd always been good to her. It said that she had always remembered that night her parents had been shot down in the street, although she'd never spoken of it and everyone assumed she'd been too young to remember. It said she'd met the Kellers and they were really nice people, whatever that meant. It concluded with:

Don't you see what's going on? All my enduring love,
Rachel

Authorities dismissed the letter as a forgery and Nathaniel's death was recorded as a heart attack. After the funeral, the police gave the note to Charles, still sealed in its evidence bag.

Not long after that, Charles's health seemed to decline at a rapid rate. He hardly ate. He refused to leave the library, scribbling things down, marking passages in various books. He was obsessed with finding something, with discovering answers to a puzzle only he seemed to comprehend. He pinned the letter most assumed his father had written to himself to the wall and surrounded it with scraps of text and pictures ripped from books he never bothered to have his wife return to the library. His face became sallow, his eyes yellow with fatigue. His wife believed he'd become schizophrenic. Many in town believed he'd always been depressed because he'd never borne a son—he couldn't relate to any of his seven daughters, and played almost no part in their lives. While others believed he'd not taken his father's death well and was deeply depressed; others still, believed he was plain crazy.

During the next few months, there were several tragedies in town. Herman Mankiewicz locked himself in his department store and trashed the place, slicing at his own merchandise with a knife, including a number of mannequins that were missing heads, before he appeared to have cut himself— perhaps an accident during his frenzy—and bled to death before he was discovered the next day by one of his employees. Bradley Cohen, a bright and promising first-grader, drowned in a puddle in the street, although no one was sure how he'd been unable to save himself in such shallow water. Mckenzie Rowan strangled the captain of the high school football team, Jerrod "Jerry" Long, while they were having sex in his car at the top of Pike's Point, which overlooked the town. Phil Harding watched his wife pour bleach over the face of their sleeping one-year-old and then they split what was left in the bottle and drank it together.

On June 16, 1948, Darlene Upshaw reported her husband's death to the authorities. He'd been spending all his time in the basement, she said, and that was where she'd found him, hanging by a rope from one of the rafters. The death was recorded as a suicide and the case was closed. Darlene took herself and her seven daughters and they are said to have moved away because they were never heard from again. They left the mansion empty and abandoned.

CHAPTER 41
THE UPSHAW MANSION

The Upshaw Mansion was eventually sold to Lincoln and Associates, a law firm out of Phoenix, Arizona, but was never, for whatever reason, put to use and sat empty for many years. It fell into disrepair.

The mansion was occasionally considered by prospective buyers, but remained on the market for years. To the people of Mesa Rapids, it would forever be called by its original name: the Upshaw Mansion, although there hadn't been an Upshaw (that anyone knew of) living in Mesa Rapids for several decades.

The town changed. The valley corroded, from overmining and a failing economy. Those who could afford to moved atop the mesa and built an affluent, elitist community. Those who could not dug in their heels and took pride in their community, forming a haven for the hippie movement and the bohemian lifestyle.

In 1997, desperate to salvage something of their investment in the Upshaw Mansion, the law firm allowed a family of four to rent the place at a reasonable rate. They were, however, clearly psychologically unstable people, and the entire family killed themselves in the house.

Chapter 42
MESA RAPIDS

Present Day

W̲hich is to say, things had never been right in Mesa Rapids. And, once again, they had slipped out of place—a breach in the canvas of reality, a tear. A threshold had been crossed. There was something in the air that affected people in strange and surprising ways, which made them laugh and experience things they knew couldn't possibly be real. It was becoming increasingly difficult to accept the world as a rational place. If Mesa Rapids had been a person, it would have been an easy diagnosis to have her committed, and, in many ways, she was. She'd slipped from the minds of the outside world. Projects were dropped, family members forgotten. Colin—who, in the back of his mind, if he'd been willing to admit it to himself, had more of an idea what was happening than most—continued to work tirelessly on his project in the basement. Others went about their lives as normal, ignoring the strange cries they heard from the streets outside their windows, going to their jobs, taking their kids to soccer practice. Many knew people who had been killed, but what could they do? *Life must go on*, as they said. They were numb. For most, the things they saw were so bizarre they refused to acknowledge them, no longer trusted their own senses, walked with their eyes straight ahead and strangely controlled smiles tugging at their lips.

Michelle Cardigan, who lived in one of the ritzier

neighborhoods on The Hill—who had never quite lived down her high school nickname: "Sweater Puppy"—had been losing things. It had started with a set of diamond earrings that had been her mother's. She'd been in a panic for a week, never finding them. Then her car keys had disappeared and her husband had been furious with her. Then she'd sat down to watch her soaps and when the commercials had come on, she'd looked down and half of the poker chips from her husband's set he'd left on the coffee table were gone. She'd been eating them. Later, she sat down for the next episode with a box of razor blades.

Nine-year-old Carrie Anderson, spending her summer vacation down by the river, avoiding her parents and new baby brother, found a small terrier among the damp and discarded leaves beneath a bush. The dog was hurt, its white and wiry hair clumped with blood, unable to lift itself. Carrie spent the next few days caring for the dog, bringing it scraps of chicken to eat, cleaning it, and the dog told her secrets. The dog told her what was happening in Mesa Rapids. The dog told her what she could do about her baby brother, how she could make him stop crying forever with a pillow. In her dreams the dog was a huge beast. Through teeth caked with blood, it spoke to her.

Harvey Glenhirsch was on the set of a new sitcom called *Meet the Newmans*, being filmed in what he thought of as the "bumfuck town of Mesa Rapids." He hadn't been sleeping well and everything annoyed him. He agreed with his agent: *Meet the Newmans* was never going to be picked up by the network, but, fresh out of anger management, it was the best his agent could do for him at the moment. He'd been having dreams about little bubbling things hiding in dark corners. When the "blond fuck," who was the director on set, pushed him too far, he attacked him with a knife. "Cut!" the director screamed, and that's exactly what he did.

The father of Zach's friend Bud got a call from the police telling him they'd found Bud's body. Bud's dad went directly to his workshop in the garage, flicked the table saw to life, and dropped his wrists over the spinning blade.

In the bedroom on the other side of the house, Bud's mother smiled. She knew better. Sometimes Bud came to her, slipped into the bed next to her while she slept. She cradled his tiny boy's body. She ran her hands down his cold back. She patted the back of his sticky head. She loved her son—she loved Bud so much! Stickiness filled her hands.

Bud's parents' bodies were never found.

And Les and Cass decided to crash another party at the Upshaw Mansion, this time just the two of them.

When they got there, they began to explore the house and were soon lost in a vast hallway. Every door they opened led to an identical, featureless room. When they finally found a window, the sun was shining outside, as if they'd wandered those halls the entire night and still couldn't find a way out.

And James Conroy saw worms wriggling beneath the skin of his arm until he cut them out with a knife and then the red worms were all over the floor.

And Tom, one of Jeremy's friends, after seeing the sculpture in Colin's room, went home after the party the night before and chugged an entire bottle of antifreeze after scooping his eyeballs out with a cake knife.

And Layla Gilbertson, Jeremy's secret lover, after hearing the son she never saw was dead—floating in a liquid haze of booze and tranquilizers— heard a tap-tap at the door of her trailer park home. "Someone's here to see me," she said, getting up as if in a dream. She opened the door and her son was crouched on the steps, looking up at her. "RayRay?" She embraced her son. "What happened, RayRay? Tell me what happened to you." He told her, his face pale, his eyes clear and shining. He told her through purple lips. He took her pain away and she drifted into comfortable warmth, a deliciously fetid swamp, wriggling with slimy life.

And Jeremy showed up with some beer and a bottle of Jack, and found Layla naked on the couch in the murk of her trailer, her pasty folds and heavy breasts beckoning. "Come here, bitch," Jeremy said. He stripped and went to her, buried himself in her flesh. She grabbed him, clawed his back. He brought his mouth to hers and it was as if his entire face was being swallowed in her mouth, wet and slippery, slimy. She clutched him and brought him into her and he thrust forward blindly, deliciously. He was inside her and it was warm and she sloshed beneath him. They sloshed together. He could already feel his approaching orgasm. She was so warm down there and encompassing. She swallowed everything he had. He pulled his head up. He opened his eyes and looked down and her face was like a glob of sagging dough. His entire bottom half was inside her. He was rocking in her fluids. The stench made his gorge rise, but he swallowed it back. He was close. So warm.

When Jeremy came, it was like nothing he'd ever experienced, his entire body racked with pleasure, melting through him, and he sank, sank into the warmth, into the slurry, and it was too much for him and he lost consciousness. And when he awoke, he was on the floor in a sticky reek, Layla gone. He vomited, picked himself up, and left.

And Paul Dumphrey, a door-to-door salesman, was sure the birds were watching him. Wherever he went, the birds, roosting in the trees or on the power lines, swiveled their heads to track his progress. When he got home, he fetched the gun he kept in a drawer in the kitchen, loaded it, and went outside. The birds immediately began to swarm. He could see them filling the sky, coming for him. He ran. He ran and ran until he was in the forest and the trees were filled with birds and he used the gun to free himself from their cawing laughter forever.

And Detective Reynolds said, "What is this shit, Sergeant?"

"These are the pics we took, Reynolds. I don't know what you're going to make of all this, but here you go. I wouldn't want your job right now."

"All this came from the Groveshaw ranch?"

"That's right."

"What's this one? Looks like something out of a John Carpenter movie."

"Well, maybe you oughta go out there and have a look for yourself then."

"But I'm still trying to sort out this Thompson family business and—"

"Have you finished your report on Paul Dumphrey?"

"What? Oh, no, not yet. That one too. I still have to—"

"And we need the paperwork on Ethan Hobb."

"Yes. Of course. What's this? Are those fingers?"

"Keep up the good work, Detective."

"Good work? I'm completely swamped, Sergeant. Where's that help you promised me? You forget I'm the only detective in this lazy-ass town."

"…"

"Sergeant?"

"I tried…"

"And?"

"Well, I called but I can't get a hold of anybody."

"What do you mean?"

"I mean, the phones aren't working."

"The phones have been working fine. I haven't—"

"Have you tried calling outside of town?"

"I don't think so."

"Just…don't worry about it right now, okay?"

"Sergeant?"

"Yeah?"

"What the fuck is going on?"

"I don't know. It was never this bad. I was just a kid the last time this happened, but my dad used to talk about it. He thought it was the Upshaws, but the Upshaws are gone. He must have been wrong. It must be something else."

"What are you talking about? What's…? Fuck. I gotta tell you, Sergeant, I'm damn tired. I spent the entire night talking with my wife."

"Your wife? When did you remarry?"

"I never have. Too busy."

"But she's been…"

"Yup. That's right."

"What'd you talk about?"

"The past. Our son. We reminisced, what can I say?"

"Reynolds, you're telling me—"

"Except there was something not right about her. She looked like my wife, but…I don't know. She wanted to show me something. I didn't go with her, was too scared, but she said she'd come back tonight."

"This is a crazy conversation, you know that?"

"Yeah. I know."

"I guess when you've seen what we have, you get a little numb to things after a while."

"Sergeant?"

"Yeah?"

"What in the blazing fuck are we talking about?"

"Nothing, Detective."

And Allen Munroe, Zach's father, was spending a lot of time at a new bar that had opened up down the street from the Upshaw Mansion. The bar was tiny and nameless, as far as Allen could tell, but every night, as darkness closed over the place, Steve, his brother who had died many years ago in the army, came and sat with him at the bar and they drank.

And Kevin Conners, a second-grader, whose backyard dumped out into a strip of land filled with scraggly trees against the highway, was out looking for bottles for his collection when he found, with a jolt of excitement, a strange-looking bottle with a cork stopper. When he pulled the stopper free, he discovered the bottle was filled with a dark crimson liquid with a strangely metallic smell. It couldn't be blood, could it? He hid the bottle and the next day, after school, went looking for more. He found several test tubes and a beaker, with similar stoppers, filled with the same substance. He was thrilled, because mostly his collection consisted of beer and soda bottles and these were a rare find, but they made him uneasy. He dumped the liquid inside them down the drain in the sink in the garage and washed them out the best he could. He tucked them away so his parents wouldn't see them and start asking questions. A few days later, the crimson fluid began to come up from the pipes, filling all the sinks in the house, the bathtub, and the toilet, then spilling over onto the floor. Then the sprinkler system came to life and painted the front lawn red.

And then it rained one morning in mid-July and it didn't stop for several days and people stayed indoors, many using the storm as an excuse not to go into work. And little Haley Meyers walked out into the rain without telling her parents, tripped, and drowned in three inches of water. And no one bothered to call the police anymore. And the parties were getting progressively heavier in the Lizard Kingdom at the art house, Maddie hiding in her room with her dog, Isabel, wishing Colin would come home. And Jeremy said, "We're all one big happy, dysfunctional family," with a strained smile and was drinking like he never had before, not talking to anyone. And Lauren was still missing. And Zach continued to see Mr. M from time to time. And parties at the Upshaw Mansion became constant, people coming and going as they pleased, always music and lights. And somewhere, from a balcony high above, Klimt looked down on Mesa Rapids, and could see there was leakage, blotting the canvas, soaking through like crimson paint.

And people had nightmares they dismissed as dreams.

PART FOUR

PAINT

"Yet, there's one point that troubles me: that human life's so short, and art is long."

—Mephistopheles, from Johann Wolfgang von Goethe's *Faust*, Stuart Atkins translation

CHAPTER 43

COLIN

When Colin completed his project with Mr. Klimt, he returned to the house and tapped on Maddie's window with his fingernail. When Maddie saw it was him, she rushed to open the window, and embraced him before he had finished climbing all the way up into her room. "I missed you. Where have you been? I missed you so much!"

"Look," Colin said, "I'm sorry," and he showed her what was in his knapsack.

Maddie started. "Where...? What did you do?" Colin grinned. "I got paid."

"Oh, my god. Colin!"

"Yeah, I know. Will you come with me?"

"With you? Where?"

"I'm getting the fuck out of this town," Colin said. "This place is no good. I want you to come with me."

Maddie looked at Colin closely. "Yes, but where?"

"Does it matter?"

Maddie thought hard about it. She sat back on the bed and something stirred in the sheets. "I suppose not."

Colin hadn't noticed the little white dog sleeping peacefully on the bed. Maddie carefully lifted the ball of fluff and placed it in her lap.

"What do you think?"

Maddie looked up at Colin and her eyes were bright. "Okay. Let's get the fuck out of here. But only if my dog can come with us."

Colin smiled.

And so they packed what few possessions they owned, tied them down in the back of Colin's truck, crossed the train tracks, and jostled out of town. Maddie left Jeremy behind without speaking another word to him and Colin turned away from the Upshaw Mansion and never looked back. They left Mesa Rapids without regrets, and felt nothing but relief.

They traveled west, because it seemed a likely direction for them to go in, taking turns with the driving, Isabel sitting calmly between them, her tiny pink tongue peeking from her mouth. They stayed a few days in Las Vegas, but soon discovered neither of them was much interested in all those lights and all that noise, and so they moved on. From there, they stayed a night in San Bernardino and then began to head north up the western coast of California. They stopped frequently and often and they found themselves smiling a lot at each other, Maddie with her hair worn straight and long down her shoulders.

They lingered in the Redwood Forest, taking pictures of the giant, prehistoric trees, pulling the truck over to admire the road tunnels carved through some of the largest ones. They laughed and Isabel barked excitedly at them, prancing and circling. They walked to a secluded spot and spread a blanket on the forest floor and ate lunch, not talking much, having no use for words, just looking around, content with each other in such a magical place. They made love beneath the trees while Isabel slept on a corner of the blanket, lifting her eyes to slits to peer at them, then letting them slide slowly shut again, as if to say: *Humans are weird, but these two are okay, I guess.*

They continued on, crossing the state line into Oregon, then took Interstate 5 until they reached Portland. It seemed like a natural place for them to go. A lot of young people were going to Portland, especially artist types like themselves. They knew, even before they reached their destination, once there, they'd be welcome and comfortable.

They found a small apartment together and spent their days exploring their new city. They hung out in cafés and had dinner with a couple from their building and when Colin began to paint again, so did Maddie.

When Maddie missed her period, she was afraid to tell Colin, and hid the positive pregnancy test at the bottom of her underwear drawer. They'd only been in Portland for a couple of weeks and already the money was almost gone. But when she did finally show the test to Colin, he only smiled, put his hand on her knee, and said, "It's okay. I love you." She'd blushed and been surprised to hear herself returning the sentiment.

They both got barista jobs at Coffee Heaven, a local coffee house owned by a young guy called Marco, with long blond hair and not much older than they were. Marco was happy to have Maddie working as long as she could, and as she ballooned, he began to joke about baby names, calling out random and ridiculous options throughout the workday: "Boris! How about Boris if it's a boy? Or Ezekiel! Go biblical, man!" And Maddie would laugh and Colin would shake his head and say, "No way. This one's special."

"You're absolutely right about that," Marco would say, putting his hand out to pat Maddie's stomach. "This little one's joining our Coffee Heaven family. He or she needs the right name." Then he'd pause,

"How about Millicent! Millicent if it's a girl!"

On a cool but clear April night, after only two hours of labor, the baby slipped crying into the world. It was a boy, six pounds and eight ounces, healthy and normal. He had a sticky mat of dark hair and his skin was red and smooth. Maddie held their new son resolutely while Colin fought back tears over her shoulder. They named him James. James Owen Thorne.

"James?" Marco said when he heard. "*That's* the name you chose?" But he had a huge grin on his face.

As James grew, his hair remained black, his eyes a deep hazel, despite his mother's naturally auburn and his father's scrappy blond hair. He was an easygoing kid, enjoyed playing with his blocks and loved the *Star Wars* movies. He was intelligent, found school easy and spent most of his free time either playing video games or talking about them.

Colin became the assistant manager at Coffee Heaven and Maddie stayed home with their son. They looked into daycare so they could both continue to work, but it was too expensive so one of them had to stay home; Maddie volunteered. They didn't have much money, but they got by okay. Maddie kept her canvas and paints set up in a corner of their apartment and managed to work on her art a few minutes here and there.

When James was in the fourth grade, Marco suddenly announced he was leaving Portland. "I gotta move on, man. I gotta see the world while I'm still young." He left the management of Coffee Heaven to Colin, and suddenly Colin and Maddie had enough money to pay their bills and make payments on a new used car and even to put a little away each month.

After Maddie sold her first painting and was then featured in galleries all over town, they put a down payment on their first house, a modest colonial with a front lawn and spacious backyard, including two apple trees: both golden delicious. They even had a white picket fence, until Maddie painted it purple. Isabel was almost sixteen at that point and spent most of her days sleeping peacefully, moving to soak in the sun from the windows as it crawled across the floor, but, with all their new yard space, they were able to get another dog: Charlie, a two-year-old chocolate lab that came from the local animal shelter. Isabel tolerated Charlie's boisterousness, ignored it, and went back to sleep.

By the time James entered middle school he was taller than both his parents. He'd grown his black hair out so that he had to keep brushing it back from his eyes. He'd met new friends at school and his grades were beginning to slip. Maddie suspected he was smoking marijuana, but Colin insisted he was too young to be exposed to such things.

One night, Colin insisted he make dinner. When Maddie asked him why, he shrugged, gave a sly look, and said he had a "big announcement." At dinner, Colin opened a bottle of wine, raised his glass and stood. "Okay. I can't wait." He looked at his family, at beautiful Maddie, her eyes wide and expectant, at James, his hair in his face, giving a teenager's smirk. "I bought out Marco," he said. "We now officially own Coffee Heaven and I've been working with some people to open another location downtown!"

"Oh, my god," Maddie said. A chilling blast of wind rocked

the flowers at the center of the table. "What does this mean?"

"It means you can buy that Maserati you've always wanted." Maddie laughed. And James, his hair pushed up away from his glowing eyes by the freezing black wind, stood, seemed to float suddenly. James lifted a knife and slammed it into the side of Maddie's neck with savage glee.

He grinned as blood pumped out over his hand. "Hi, Colin. Did you miss me?"

"James! What have—"

"James? Did I tell you my name was James? That was a lie. I'm Derek. Your old friend. You remember me, don't you, stupid fuck? What's your name? What the *fuck* is your name?"

But that's not how things happened.

Colin jumped awake, his entire body humming. He'd fallen asleep again. He groaned, his back throbbing painfully, and rolled to his side. He was in the ancient recliner that only lay partially flat, with springs that dug into your back. He was in the basement—at Klimt's house. He was cold. He hugged himself, shivering, before he realized it was actually warm in the basement. Warm and stuffy. He blinked at the wall of shadowy junk across from him: he did not feel sane; had, at times, begun to believe the fantasies that spun through his head. They were real to him. He could see Maddie's face, red and straining, as she gave birth to their son; could see the wrinkly baby James, could see how his eyes lit up when he came home from school with a straight-A report card to show off. He could see himself leaving Mesa Rapids, giving it the finger as his truck jostled over the rise and Maddie laughed good-naturedly. He had *not* seen what was actually on the other side of that rise; he had *not* seen himself driving down and back into Mesa Rapids. He had *not* seen Jeremy raise his foot and stomp, and stomp down on the baby, crushing its life and its future from it, and stomp over and over again.

The door above creaked, and someone entered the basement.

Colin jumped to his feet, glanced around. He had papers and various things spread all over the floor, boxes pulled out and tipped over, that he'd been rummaging through. His notes, sketches, notebooks were everywhere. He'd tacked torn pages all over a large corkboard he'd found, taped others over the surface of half a Ping-Pong table. A sketch he couldn't remember drawing but was clearly his style, of a jar spilling muck crawling with faces, caught his eye. He glanced at the huge concrete wall he'd cleared everything away from, at the pathetic outlines he'd begun to paint there, and made a face.

Klimt stood at the top of the rickety stairs looking down on him. There was amusement on his face. "How are you, Colin?"

Colin blinked the crustiness from his eyes. "Fine."

"That's good. I want you to be fine." Klimt began to come down the stairs, slowly. He wore his bluish sport coat, pleated pants, shiny black shoes. "I won't ask you to show me *what* you're working on. I came only for assurance that you continue to work. Of course, you must rest from time to time, I understand. And your midnight excursions are excusable. I need only to know my money is being well-spent."

Colin wiped sweat from his forehead. "Uh. Yeah. I'm doing what I can."

Klimt stopped at the bottom of the stairs. "I see you've begun to dig for inspiration," he said, pointing his chin at the overturned boxes and the junk strewn about.

"That's just—"

Klimt raised his hand. "Exactly what you should be doing. I'm glad you've found a haven down here." He took several steps into the basement and turned to face the concrete wall Colin had cleared. "Is this to be the final mural?"

Colin looked at the wall. "Yes, I think so. I mean, if that's okay."

"Perfect. But you'll need a method to reach the top, no great feat of engineering like Michelangelo required, but something. Have you found a ladder down here?"

"I hadn't looked. I—"

"You will. I am sure of it. I have complete confidence in your abilities to see this thing through. Well, I'll let you get back to it." Klimt walked back to the stairs and began to climb upward.

"Mr. Klimt?"

Klimt stopped, halfway to the top. "You may call me Harold,

if you like. I believe we've been acquainted long enough now."

"Yeah, sure. Okay—Harold? Why am I doing this?"

Klimt looked over his shoulder. "Why do we do anything? What is artistic expression worth?"

"Yes, but why do you want a mural down here in this dark basement where no one is ever gonna see it?"

Klimt smiled. "Oh, this is much more than a basement. This is the Upshaw Mansion. This spot is history."

"What if I didn't want to do this anymore?"

Klimt's smile dropped from his face. "Am I not paying you enough?"

"No it's not—"

"Then I'll double your fee, but I don't want to hear another word about it." Klimt flew up the last of the stairs. At the top, he turned back, leaning on the railing, his smile returning. "Remind me to tell you about my first job as an artist. You may be surprised to discover we have more in common than you think."

The door creaked, shut, and Colin was once more alone in the basement of the Upshaw Mansion with the shadows and the quiet.

CHAPTER 44

I can't really put my finger on it, that's the problem. I know there's something wrong. It can't just be that I'm not sleeping well. I always feel this way when I can't sleep and I have a lot of bad dreams, unsure of everything, scared. I've tried to dismiss my doubts in the knowledge that Klimt is a crazy, old eccentric, but that assurance is not enough. And yet, what harm is it to paint a mural for an old man? It's just a painting, and the money, when I finish, will be enough to escape this shithole town, take Maddie with me, start a new life. I have to keep pushing myself. I can't let the outside world steal my focus. The sooner I finish, the sooner I can go home.

There are things from my dreams I've begun to paint: creatures, wailing faces. It's what Klimt wants me to do. He wants me to set loose my imagination. He says truly great art, the kind that is remembered, that immortalizes its artists, comes from a deep and abstract place; he says that place is greater than ourselves, that we must invoke it. He wants me to ignore my intellectual mind, turn it off. He wants me not to concern myself with questions or rationalities. His advice is insistent, and it's this insistence that troubles me.

The other day, at Elephant House, I told Donnie about my dreams. "Sounds inspiring," he said, grinning. "But, of course, there's inspiration all around you, isn't there?"

I wonder what he meant by that? I mean, I know in a general sense, everything an artist comes in contact with is inspiration, blah, blah. But that's not exactly what he was saying. Because I know the subject of my mural: it's darkness, the underworld—hell. It's meant to be twisted and disturbing. A perfect subject for a basement. It's that sort of thing. It's about things ugly and horrible, within us all. Is that what Donnie was saying? Why does that bother me? I need sleep, need to sleep.

When I asked Donnie what he meant, he only laughed, told me he had to go. He stood and limped across the bar to the door. "That one in the corner's not bad," he said over his shoulder, but I was in no mood for hitting on anyone, for the hollowness of the one-night stand. It was too easy, at least at Elephant House. Everyone is so lonely. You can see it in their eyes. And then Donnie was gone and I was the only one left sitting at the bar.

Chapter 45

ZACH

Zach watched the boy struggling in the dirt through a narrow slit in his bedroom curtains. The boy was flailing his arms, punching out with his fists, twisting about. Zach didn't know who the boy was, had never seen him before. The boy fell, scraping his knees, and screamed.

Zach couldn't see what the boy was fighting, but he knew something was there because he'd used his *Is this a dream?* card—he was *not* dreaming. He knew the card worked because he'd used it earlier, when he'd been drifting on a boat with someone who wouldn't show his face, and all he could hear was muttering. And when the boat had drifted into a smelly bog and the person had begun to turn, slowly and deliberately, like a dead person, and he'd been so terrified he'd almost forgotten the card was in his pocket; and when the tip of the dead man's nose, green and contorted, began to come into view, he'd finally remembered, and ripped the card from his pocket: *Is this a dream?* He'd known then that he was asleep and he'd woken up with a jolt and heard himself say aloud to his empty room in the middle of the night: "Don't you see what's going on?"

Except he didn't know what was going on. He knew people were acting funny all over town. There were a lot of missing kids at his school, including several from his class, and even some of the teachers. One kid from his class, Henry Morgan, had told him Mrs. Jennings, one of the fifth-grade teachers, was dead. He said she'd jammed a fork in a light socket.

But the thought that made Zach's heart go cold was that no one seemed worried about it, no one was doing anything. People's attitudes were wrong. Henry, when he'd told him about Mrs. Jennings, had only shrugged, like it was normal for a teacher to die, like kids disappearing every day and never being heard from again was an okay thing. It gave him goose pimples just thinking about it.

The boy flipped and landed hard on his back. Zach could tell the air had been knocked out of him. The boy kicked, tried to stand, was knocked down again.

Just because Zach couldn't see what the boy grappled with, he knew, did not mean it wasn't there. No one could see Mr. M at the edge of the playground either, but Zach could. And Zach knew Mr. M was dangerous. He'd seen Mr. M open his briefcase for Bud. He knew Mr. M had done something to his best friend, and that no one would ever see him or his parents again. He saw Mr. M every day, but he was too terrified to confront him, wouldn't even go into the playground at recess anymore, stayed at the top of the hill, close to the teachers. But his precautions weren't enough, and he didn't feel safe no matter what he did. Every day Mr. M was there, staring at him, challenging him, but not moving any closer— why? He knew Mr. M was involved in what was going on around town, but what could he do? He was scared, and it made him mad.

A vision had been going through his head, the familiar icy crust settling over his brain, playing over and over. He knew it was important, but he didn't know why. Who were these people? He kept seeing a woman, in a formfitting red dress, with flowing blonde hair, marching on the Upshaw Mansion, a giant hammer she could barely lift clutched with both hands. Then the woman was surrounded by large, dancing shadows with indistinguishable faces. He saw another woman, young and pretty, with one of these shadows just over her shoulder, oblivious to the black claws closing over her throat. He saw a face in one of the basement windows, level with the ground, a look of terror, striking the unbreakable glass with blood-pulped fists. He saw a man in fancy clothes and shiny shoes dancing a subdued jig. And he knew they were all scared of this dancing man. And he was standing with the others, the blonde woman on one side of him, the pretty one on the other. The man he'd met in the Upshaw Mansion, Colin—who had saved him, who had given him the *Is this a dream?* card— was standing next to the pretty woman. They were all looking into the shadows, where Mr. M lurked, and they could all see Mr. M. The blonde woman was angry and the pretty woman was scared. But the man from the Upshaw Mansion was something else, and the scariest part of his vision, the part that really chilled Zach, was the laughter coming from Colin. It was insane and unbearable. That laughter followed Zach into his waking life—he could hear it, even now.

Somehow he knew these people were important. They weren't blind to Mr. M. They could see him, just like Zach could. That had to mean something, right?

The face in the basement window was his. A shudder ran through him.

Things were seriously wrong in Mesa Rapids. People were passive, drugged, like a surgeon had gassed them, preparing them to go under, to wake up changed, with things missing, cut out and arrayed on a tray in pooling blood. Zach was worried. Something nagged him, at the back of his mind…

The boy. Shouldn't he be concerned with the boy outside his window? Shouldn't he help him? Shouldn't he call the police or something?

The thought surfaced in his head—not for the first time, but its persistence was becoming difficult to ignore, like something ugly coming up briefly for air—that he was going to have to do something. Just like when Bud had gone missing. Only this time, he couldn't fail. This time, it was for the fate of the entire town of Mesa Rapids.

Should he call Colin, who'd given him the *Is this a dream?* card? Should he call the man with the crazy laugh in his vision? He shook his head.

He didn't have a choice—he had to do this on his own.

Outside the window, the boy was on the ground, his limbs contorted in awkward positions. There was blood and Zach could hear the snapping of bones.

A couple minutes later, he heard his father storm into the house, slam the door, the entire place shaking with violence and sorrow.

CHAPTER 46

*f*ind myself inside a strange building made of glass. A glass stairway spirals beneath my feet. Condensation beads the surface of every-thing, making my descent slippery, rivulets of moisture running lines down the glass walls. The glass is solid and unbreakable and thick so that only a vague and milky notion of the outside world is visible. The air reeks of excrement, mildew, and curdled emotions.

At the bottom of the stairs, there is a small balcony that overlooks a vast enclosed room. From there, I can see, filling most of the room so that people have to walk over it, lies a monstrous beast spilled about and breathing, its anatomy like connected lumpen piles of gut-filled sacks coming to a drooping face and huge toothless mouth, open and waiting. The glass structure seems to be built around this creature—this god—so that its tail end sags outside in the colorful daylight, the majority of its bulk, however, lying within the grayness of the interior. Below, I know, distends the beast's belly, dropping infinitely into the cavernous deep, and there are people in there, swallowed and floating helplessly, doomed to dissolve in the murk for eternity.

Everywhere people mill about, dressed in clothes stained and ragged from too much wear. Several of them surround the head of the Great Beast, contemplating its gaping mouth. Some of them are even attempting to communicate with it, discussing their lives, attempting to discern their possible fate, although the Great Beast can only nod and roll its eyes ineffectually.

I am trapped with these people. The only way out is down the gullet of the Great Beast. I watch as someone, having finally worked up enough courage, steps up before the Great Beast's mouth and lunges into it. *The mouth snaps shut and the woman is quickly swallowed. I watch her, through the thin membrane of the Great Beast's body, sliding through the misshapen gullet, bobbing for a moment in the stomach, and then beginning through the intestinal tract. The woman makes a sound, a contented sigh muffled through the wads of flesh, and disappears, apparently passing through to the outside, shitted into the Garden on the other side.*

I understand then, I have a choice. I can choose to remain in this monotonous and muggy staleness for as long as I like—there are others who seem to have been here for a long time, hundreds, perhaps thousands of years—or I can take my chances with the Great Beast. It appears that some are passed through to the other side, while others sink horribly into the juices of that bottomless stomach, forever mired in the slow-burning pain of the Great Beast's digestive acids. Yet no one seems to know what the Great Beast's criteria for judgment are. Do those who have lived virtuous and benevolent lives pass through, while those who have been cruel and callous sink into the stomach? Or is judgment based on some other means? On belief? On the repentance of sins?

I awaken, drenched in icy sweat, immediately take myself to my mural and begin to paint.

CHAPTER 47
LAUREN

Lauren spread jam on some Club crackers she'd found in the back of the pantry and ate without tasting. She didn't have much food left in the house, but she had enough, she told herself, to last quite some time if she was careful. Shadows caroused in the corners of the kitchen and living room even though it was the middle of the day; she had the shades drawn tight. Sometimes she heard people screaming outside, but there was nothing she could do. She shivered through her robe, always cold, the heat no longer working.

She'd tried to get out in time. She'd tried to leave Mesa Rapids behind. She'd known. She didn't know how, but she'd known something horrible was happening to her hometown. She'd tried to get her boyfriend to go with her. Poor Mark. She could see his face... And her father...all those people at the ranch...

Her mouth let out a sound, something like a bark of laughter, and she cringed. She hadn't had time to be sad or grieve. She was too scared. She took her crackers and darted down the hallway, heading back to the downstairs bedroom, where she'd been hiding out. She sunk into a chair and ate a few more crackers. She'd once been a writer and editor of a well-respected art magazine, a long time ago, in another life, and look at her now. What had happened to her? What had become of her town?

She'd tried to drive away, tried to escape. She'd come around a bend in the road and seen what she'd seen and she'd been so terrified she'd turned her truck around and tried to go another way, but soon she'd been lost. She'd wound through some more trees and come over another rise and there, somehow, had been the same sight. She'd tried another route, coming around a bend where something had darted across the road, but it had only been Mark, sitting with his back against a tree, his car pulled over to the side of the road, door open, beeping mutedly in the denseness of the air.

She'd pulled her own truck over, left the engine running, and stepped out. Mark's shoulders hadn't moved; he'd made no sound of having heard her approach. He was facing away from her, looking out over the hill. Lauren had felt herself shaking, her legs shuddering as she lifted them awkwardly with each step, fear surrounding her like an oppressive fog.

"Mark?" she'd called out to him, but not too loudly, as she hadn't wanted to attract unwanted attention from the forest. "Mark, it's Lauren." She'd been hardly able to feel her feet touching the ground, hardly breathing, holding her breath.

The foliage beneath her seemed to writhe and shudder.

Even as she'd reached him, she'd been able to see he was sitting on a rock against the tree, a rock that gave him a view of what was over the hill. "Mark?" she'd said. "Please?" She'd reached out and touched his shoulder. He'd slumped, fallen toward her, his face rolling over into view.

She'd clasped a hand over her mouth. "Whaaa…" She'd repressed a scream. He'd still been warm, but no longer alive. She couldn't imagine what had made his face like that. She'd stepped away, and the sight over the hill had come into view, the sight she'd turned her truck away from over and over. It wasn't the lake of blood. It wasn't that horrible, yet it filled her heart with dread. Mesa Rapids had loomed at the bottom of the rise.

She'd run back to her truck, gunned the engine up and down the road. She'd driven all the way home, through the streets without looking around, pulled into the circling driveway of her house, killed the engine, and gone inside. Instinct had led her to the kitchen, where she'd grabbed the largest knife from the wooden block on the counter and stepped outside. She'd bent down and drawn the knife through the dirt in the flower bed. Blood had welled into the cut. She'd dropped the knife, gone back inside, and immediately drawn the blinds closed.

Now days had passed, and she knew the truth. Mesa Rapids was sick, the earth diseased, and Mr. Klimt in the Upshaw Mansion had something to do with it. She was terrified. Even now she was crying. What could she do? But already she knew the time for despair was passing, and the strength within her, the strength passed down from her father, the strength that she'd used to build success in her business and personal lives, was rising up, and she knew she couldn't keep hiding. If she couldn't escape it, she had to confront the source of her torment, the source of the disease that had come to her hometown.

She had to kill Harold Klimt.

CHAPTER☐48

I woke up and there was a lot more of the mural done than I remember doing. How can that be? I'm having blackouts, losing my grip on reality.

I get so lonely I wander the house sometimes. I spent a couple of hours talking with a jovial fat man who claimed to be a wealthy art collector. He grinned at me, adjusted his tie, and said I should see his house. "The extravagance," he said. "You'd love it." His name was Ethan Hobbs and he was obviously a lecherous gay man, so when he invited me to join him in one of the bedrooms with a slanted smirk, I declined as politely as I could, and hurried away.

There is a woman I've been spending time with who has been hanging around in one of the lounge rooms. She smiles kindly at me as soon as she notices me walking up to her. She likes to lay out on one of the couches where the sunlight strikes her bare, milky ankles and rises up her body, warming her from toe to head by mid-morning. She's been up there, waiting for me, the past couple of days. We don't talk about much. She says the weather outside is getting colder. When I asked her to tell me a bit about herself, she only smiled that lazy smile and said her story was too long, "and not very interesting, I'm afraid." I didn't push her further and sat across from her and I think I dozed for a little while.

I'm tired. I'm very tired. I no longer have any idea how much sleep I've been getting.

The other night, out at Elephant House, Donnie pointed me toward a woman who was crying quietly to herself in the corner. When I hesitated, Donnie said, "Trust me. I'm your friend. You'll make her feel better. I'm your friend." So I went over to her, introduced myself. When she didn't wave me away, I sat down across from her. I put my hands out on the table and it was easy, she clasped me tight and began to tell me all about her boyfriend, how he hit her, how she'd been pregnant and they'd been in a fight and she'd fallen and had a miscarriage. I told her I was sorry. I told her that really was a tragic story. She cried and said I was very kind, said I was a good listener. She asked me to walk her home.

Back at her place, she attacked me, kissed me furiously. She grabbed me and hauled me to her bedroom. She told me to rip her clothes off, not to unbutton or unzip anything, that she wanted to hear the fabric tear. She wanted me to tie her up. She bucked beneath me. Then she called me stupid, said I should hit her, said she liked that. I ignored her and pounded her hard, getting ready to come, but when I was almost there, she leaned up and spat in my face, in my eye. I recoiled, stung. "What the fuck?" I said.

"Hit me. Hit me." And I was so close, I couldn't stop. I gave her a backhand across the face and she cackled. I smacked her, and I smacked her again. I came, flopping out, spurting across her belly. I stumbled away, my legs awkward and numb. I looked at her, tied by her wrists and ankles, squirming on her back. My heart was beating a mile a minute. When I'd caught my breath, I bent down to untie one of her wrists, but she screamed at me. "No!" she said. "Hit me! Hit me, you fucking pussy!" I fought to untie her, but she continued to scream. She spat in my face again, this time splattering her fizzing spittle in my other eye. I was pissed. I could feel the anger rising up in me like some sort of burning ember, like a brand on my heart.

"Fine! Fuck you!" I snatched up my clothes and headed for the door.

"No, wait!" she called after me.

"Nobody knows I'm here!" I laughed, slamming the door on my way out.

But that didn't really happen. That was just one of my dreams.

I wish I hadn't given away the Is this a dream? card to that kid. At the time I'd thought I wouldn't need it. I'd thought I'd be fine after I caught a few hours of sleep. I looked out the window the other day and I saw the boy walking by on the sidewalk. He stopped and he saw me peering out at him from the basement window. He stared for a second, then ran away. It wasn't until he was gone I realized he looked exactly like I had looked at that age. He wore my face.

It's just that sometimes I'm working on the mural and then I drift off, brush still in hand. When I wake up, there's a long smudge running down the wall I have to fix, or else it seems I've been painting in my sleep. It's like the time when I was very young and my mother told me a scary story before bedtime. I remember it well.

In the story, it is nighttime on every page and the illustrated trees look sickly yet alive. A young boy wanders through those woods alone, when he hears something behind him, a snapping twig. He is scared, and starts to run. On the next page, we see what pursues him. It is a strange pair of green pants; just pants, no legs, but something about the opening about the waist implies much more, forming a mouth of sorts, gibbering. The boy runs and he is pursued. On each page the boy struggles through a different nightmare landscape: a swamp where faces stare up at him from the muck, trees with mossy branches reaching out for him, reptilian animals with grins of triumph. Until eventually, the boy sees his village before him. He runs to it, and waiting by the gates, springing out at him, tackling him to the ground, is the pair of green pants.

On the next page, the boy walks happily through town, wearing his new green pants, showing them off. And there's a moral to the story, although it escapes me at the moment. The boy has gained a new friend. Something like that. The problem is, the boy's face always seemed strange to me. I remember looking at it closely. His smile was different than before, than it was at the beginning of the story. His smile looked kind of like the one made by the pants, sloppy and gibbering. And I always thought the pants had somehow swallowed the boy, and now it was those creepy green pants walking around town, morphed to look like the boy, pretending to be kind and friendly, waiting for their next victim.

That's how I remember the story, anyway. But that's crazy, right?

That just goes to show you how a kid's imagination can twist a perfectly innocent story. All I know for sure is that I couldn't sleep for weeks. I was too scared. I'd find myself under the covers, the lights out, the door closed, and I couldn't help but imagine those green pants stalking around outside, or coming after me in my dreams if I fell asleep. What if there really were things—like those green pants—that could eat you whole, and then walk around in everyday life pretending to be normal? But they weren't normal. And all they wanted was to play their little game of eating and eating...

I went back later to make sure she was dead.

CHAPTER 49

*I*had this feeling Donnie would be able to tell me what was going on, so I tread quietly up the basement stairs, out the back door, and around the house, walking, as I often did at night, to Elephant House, down that lonely street.

It was a particularly quiet night, not a single glowing window in any of the houses, the streetlights creating pools of earthy yellow fogged with insects every other block. I could hear my sneakers padding on the pavement, old leather whining as it stretched. It was a warm night, but the breeze held a brisk chill, the smell of decaying leaves.

When I got to Elephant House, the lights were on, so I opened the door and went inside. The usual overflowing bathroom smell assaulted my nose, but I knew I'd adjust to it quickly. There was no one at the bar so I took a seat, looking at myself peeking back from the mirror between the arrays of liquor bottles. I was disappointed not to see Donnie, his hunched shoulders, turning on his bar stool to greet me with that smile, but he often came limping in right after I did. There was no sign of the bartender. I pulled my pack of cigarettes from my pocket and set it before me. I lit up, striking a match, inhaled deeply, exhaled through my nose. There was no music playing. When I turned to look behind me, all the tables were empty.

That's strange, I thought. I stood, mashed my cigarette out in one of the ashtrays. I walked around to the tables, but the place wasn't big and I could see the entire establishment from the moment I entered. I walked up to the only door in the place, which led to the back room, and pushed it open. There was a storage room that ran the length *of the bar, a sink and stacks of cartons filled with glassware. There were plain brown boxes filled with bar supplies and, at one end of the room, a door to a walk-in refrigerator. I opened the heavy insulated door and there were cases of beer in stacks, a shelf lined with liquor bottles, a box of limes, things like that. I closed the refrigerator, a chill running through me, and walked out of the bar.*

I walked down the street, my hands in my pockets. I just walked, not in any particular direction, and it was so quiet I could hear my own breathing. I sounded, to myself, as if I were breathing too hard. I was just walking. I hadn't been exerting myself in any way. I came into the spotlight from one of the street lamps, and then I was out the other side. I was going toward the house of the woman I had been with the night before, to make sure she was okay. What was her name? Janet? Julia? Judith? It wasn't far, but it was difficult to be sure which house it was in the dark.

I tried the doorbell, heard it ringing inside. No response. I expected a light to turn on, but there was nothing. I knocked. Nothing. I tried the doorknob. It turned and I stepped into the house. I looked for a light switch, but even when I found it, flicked it upward, the lights remained off. I crept through the shadowy house. I went down the hallway. The bedroom door was closed. I pushed on it, opening the door. There was no one inside the room, although I could make out the straps still hanging from the bedposts from the light through the window, so I knew it was the right house. But I didn't like being in there. I was spooked and hurried down the hall and out of the house.

My footsteps echoed on the abandoned street. I kept thinking someone was following me, but when I stopped suddenly to listen, it was dead quiet. When I looked over my shoulder, there were only those hazy spotlights, interspersed by darkness. There might have been movement distantly up the street. I walked faster. Now my breathing was labored. Now my heart was pounding. I knew then, somehow, that I was alone on the street, except for what stalked me. I knew the houses were empty. There was no one but me. I staggered, beginning to run, and the pursuit continued, whatever it was. I fled.

I kept thinking about what Donnie had said to me many times

over and over: "I'm your friend." Except now I could hear it correctly.
He hadn't said: "friend," but "fiend."

   I'm your fiend.

CHAPTER 50

COLIN

Colin awoke with a jerk. His first thought: *What the fuck?*
He lifted himself and winced as a muscle spasmed painfully in his back. He'd fallen asleep in the damn chair again. The first thing he looked at was his mural. It was coming along nicely, but he still had a lot of work to do. Then he saw the scattered papers, arranged in piles all across the floor, pulled from boxes he remembered vaguely contained letters and journals of past occupants of the Upshaw Mansion.

He heard the door above creaking open, and Mr. Klimt was smiling down on him.

For a moment, he considered the man. Everyone in Mesa Rapids wanted to meet Harold Klimt—had come to his parties hoping for a glimpse of his perfectly pressed sport coats, fresh-shined shoes, and beaming face—yet so few had ever had the chance to speak with him. Now, here Colin was, about to have *another* conversation with the illustrious figure, although he could have told anyone it was no big deal. "You know you scream in your sleep, don't you?" Klimt said, his smile unchanging. He began to slowly descend the stairs, continuing to speak without waiting for an answer from Colin. "Oh, yes. Blood curdling. Can hear you all the way through the house. I don't know how frightened by your dreams you must be, but I sympathize. I too have been inflicted with such torments. But where are my manners? "How are you?"

Colin blinked. He had no idea he screamed in his sleep. "I'm good, I guess."

"Wonderful." Klimt stepped down to the concrete floor. "Tell me, how's progress on our little project?"

Colin nodded at the wall.

Klimt came forward and looked. He brought his hand up to stroke his chin. "Yes, excellent. I believe you're beginning to see…" He let his words trail off and then he was silent.

Klimt stood looking for several minutes while Colin groped from the chair to his feet and tried to shake himself awake.

After a while, Klimt spoke. "I know part of you wants to leave," he said. "I know you're afraid. I know you have your doubts, your insecurities. But you're close, closer than you think. We have to finish it this time. We've been so close before. This time—we'll finish. This time—we'll go all the way." Klimt hung his head.

"I…I don't know what you're talking about…"

Klimt turned and looked at Colin. For a moment, his eyes remained misty, as if he were thinking of things long in the past. "I'm sorry," he said. "Why should these things matter to you? I had family, once. I was not much older than you… My daughters…" Klimt shook himself, much like Colin had done a few minutes ago, and his eyes cleared. "But I was going to tell you about my early years as an artist, wasn't I?"

"Yeah. That's what you said last time. You said you'd done something like this." Colin waved his hand at the mural. "Your first job."

"Oh, I won't tell you about my first job, but I will tell you about my most important job, the one that changed my life…"

For a second, Klimt's eyes glassed over again. Then he regained his composure and looked around the basement. "Shall we sit for a moment?" He walked over to where some of the junk was stacked, picked up a stool of sorts, and brought it back to the old recliner. He waved Colin to sit in the recliner. "Please." He sat on the stool.

Colin sat, his back groaning as it settled into the familiar position. He didn't speak.

Klimt cleared his throat. "I was in advertising, as a young man. My parents were wealthy and I was highly educated, but I chose my field for its growth potential and as a means to exercise my natural artistic abilities and aptitude with people, knowing I didn't want to be a stuffy, and woefully underpaid, university professor like my father. It was a demanding job and, as it turned out, rather stressful. I used to come home at night, completely exhausted, have a beer, a small meal, and pass out on the couch until my alarm woke me to do it all over again the next day. I was not living the life I had hoped to live. So, when the company I worked for opened a small branch in the town of Mesa Rapids, I jumped at the opportunity, knowing the job would be less demanding and I'd finally be away from the noise of the city.

"I looked in town at rental properties, and there were several available to suit my needs, but there was only one I fell in love with: the Upshaw Mansion. It had stood empty for many years, I was told, owned by a law firm of some sort, never been rented before. I was also told it had a disturbing history, but I was unconcerned with such things. I snatched at the opportunity— although you may think it strange for someone such as myself to desire as large a property as this one—the price unbelievable, compelled by something inside me to rent it.

"This was in the '90s, you see, during a time of economic confidence and prosperity. I was making a lot of money, despite myself, and I envisioned being manager of the Mesa Rapids office in only a few short years. The job, however, proved a little *slower* than I was used to. I found myself with extra time and needed something in my life to fill it.

"Like many in the advertising industry, my interest bloomed, as a young boy, from my artistic talent. I was a natural painter. I loved art classes in school. I used to paint whatever was in front of me: the house, our blue heeler Smokey, my dad in his workshop, anything I found interesting at the time. With my new job secured in Mesa Rapids, I went to the store, bought myself the finest set of paints I could find, some canvases, brushes, anything I might need, and began to paint again.

"To be honest, I hadn't thought of doing such a thing in years. There was something driving me to paint, and I welcomed it. It felt good. Soon, I was painting things less figuratively. My creations were more abstract. I began to paint things from my imagination and things from my dreams."

Klimt paused. He dropped his eyes to his hands. He took a deep breath, as if he were struggling with some sort of emotion.

"And you began to paint down here, down in the basement..." Colin said.

Klimt nodded. "Yes. You'd even find some of my marks under yours on the wall, if you were to chip deep enough. But I failed. I wasn't good enough. I wasn't the right one. My family—"

"Family?"

"Oh...yes. Have I forgotten to mention my wife and my two daughters? How silly of me. Yes, they were with me, but they were unhappy with my neglect, because, you see, I had been ignoring them. I'd failed to appear at work and been terminated and my wife was hounding me, a constant distraction from my work..."

Colin swallowed and heard an audible click in his throat. "What happened to them?"

"They're around here somewhere. They... There was an argument, I guess you could say. It was ugly. It doesn't matter, but... All that matters now is that what was started is finished. It's never been completed before, although some, throughout the years, have come close. It's all here." He waved at the basement. "You've likely seen some of the papers. I had my chance and I failed, but I've come back. I tried to pass on, to forget about this place, but I failed at that as well. I am no longer able to complete the work, so I found you. You're perfect."

Colin gaped. "But, I don't understand. I'm just..."

"You don't *need* to understand. It's like I've told you, true art comes from deep within, from a place ineffable, and we are its conduits, its mediums of expression, nothing more." Klimt stood abruptly. "Now, you must get back to work. I'm afraid things have become urgent. You must focus. Do you need more supplies? You have food? The paints I've provided are sufficient?"

"Uh, yes. I have everything I need."

"And you're happy with the compensation I am providing you?"

"Yes."

"Good." Klimt dug into his pocket and produced a small leather pouch. "Another two thousand," he said, "to assure you of my seriousness, and I will let you get back to it." He turned and walked to the stairs.

Colin watched Klimt ascend the stairs, unmoving in the recliner, numb.

When Klimt reached the top, he turned and leaned over the balcony as he'd done before. His expression was solemn, nearly unreadable. "You must finish. Now. Quickly. I can no longer allow you to leave, not until you are done. I am sorry."

Klimt stepped away from the balcony, melting into the shadows. The door closed, and there was the sound of a bolt being drawn, the lock being secured.

"Wait, but..." Colin began, but it was already too late.

The door might seem flimsy, but he knew, without even trying, it would never allow him to leave.

CHAPTER 51

A^{lone.}

Chapter 52

MADDIE

Maddie flicked the brush across the canvas, stopped, leaned her head back, and looked at what she'd done so far. She hated it. She told herself there were no mistakes. She was being abstract, painting layer upon layer to obtain depth, using techniques she'd learned in art school. But it wasn't working. She wasn't feeling it.

She set her brush down in the easel tray and looked out the window. Beyond their yard of trampled dirt, the Upshaw Mansion leered at her.

She'd been spending her evenings alone. After she got home from work, she'd heat something up in the microwave and then take Isabel out for a short walk. But Isabel's walks were becoming shorter and shorter. She didn't like it out there most evenings. She'd seen some strange things. Odd things.

She'd seen people wandering around the dog park, wearing stained bathrobes, or with their clothes torn, sleeves hanging loose, hair matted and stuck with grass as if they'd been sleeping in the park, shocked faces, distant, glassy eyes. She'd seen neighbors fighting, spouses screaming at each other on their front porches, oblivious to their neighbors' leering stares. She'd seen a young boy in a Halloween costume chase a cat with a slingshot. She'd seen puddles under the trees that, when they caught the setting sunlight just right, glinted a deep red color. She'd seen a little girl hauling a wagon loaded with shoe boxes digging holes with a gardening trowel, burying the boxes one at a time, leaving a stick jutting from the ground to mark each location.

And then there'd been the really odd things—the creepy things.

One day, a brindle dog had bounded up to her and Isabel, stopping in their path. The dog had sat, looked at her, at Isabel, and then bounded away. A few minutes later, a howl had come from very close, and when Maddie turned to look around, she'd seen dogs coming out of hiding from behind trees all over the park, twenty, perhaps thirty of them. They all looked in her direction with intelligent eyes and Isabel began to pant, to scratch anxiously at the ground. Maddie had picked up her dog and hurried home.

Another time, she'd been walking on the sidewalk—Isabel happily trotting ahead, her little white nub of a tail held high and wagging—and something had caught her eye, causing her to turn her head to look at a passing car. As the car had pulled ahead, begun to turn down the next street, she'd strained her eyes to be sure she'd been seeing what she'd thought she'd been seeing. She'd been unable to see who was driving the car, but the backseats had seemed to be piled high with large, lumpy things. They couldn't have been what she'd thought they'd been. She knew that now, because she'd thought they'd been severed heads, moldering and vacant.

At work she'd heard crazy stories. Jessie, one of her co-workers, had said her boyfriend, Jerry, had lit himself on fire and run through the streets screaming about hellfire and brimstone. She'd laughed when she'd told Maddie the story. Jerry was at the hospital now, although people said the wait times were excruciating these days.

She'd also heard there was a little girl named Becky who'd been crying blood since Tuesday of last week; that the police department now stood abandoned and empty, its doors swinging open in the wind; that there were children on the street with knives; that more elementary school kids had been found drowned in the river; that one of the famous artists from The Hill (no one seemed to know which one) had been using blood for paint; that there was now a mass grave out at Remington Cemetery, where people were happily depositing their loved ones.

Maddie, of course, didn't believe most of these rumors, and didn't trust most of what she saw, but she knew something was wrong; she could feel the *wrongness* in her gut. It felt like she was the only one who could see it, too. Everyone else seemed perfectly happy with the situation in Mesa Rapids, acted as if it were normal. People around her shrugged and said things like, "These things happen," and "Better luck next time." But Maddie knew better. People were going crazy. They weren't themselves. Something was happening. She could see that, even if they couldn't.

What if Colin's dead?

She pushed the thought away. Colin was working for Mr. Klimt in the Upshaw Mansion. He was being paid a lot of money for some sort of art project and it was probably demanding. She should let him work. He'd come home when he was ready.

What if he's in trouble?

Why would he be in trouble? All of the crazy things were happening outside and Colin was safely indoors, in probably one of the safest places in Mesa Rapids.

Do you really believe that?

No.

She did not think the Upshaw Mansion was the safest place in Mesa Rapids. She thought about the party she'd been to there, what felt like a long time ago. She remembered endless hallways and rooms. She remembered shadowy faces floating over her. She remembered a shifting maze, a terrible place.

Maddie shivered.

You should go and talk with him, make sure he's okay.

She looked past her painting and out the window again. There it was, that ugly thing: the Upshaw Mansion. It was so close. Her room was almost in its shadow. The last thing she wanted to do was go over there, especially alone.

Tap, tap.

She looked up; someone was at the door. She stood, crossed the room.

Jeremy was standing in the hallway. "Hey, Maddie," he said. "Do you want to crash Klimt's party again tonight?"

Maddie started to shake her head automatically, then stopped. "Maybe. Who's going?"

Jeremy stared at her.

"Just you and me?"

"Yes."

"Where's Les and Cass?"

Jeremy shrugged.

Maddie thought of Colin. Maybe she could find Colin. "Okay. I'll go with you."

Jeremy smiled.

"Just let me feed Isabel and get ready. I'll be right out."

"Good," Jeremy said, and walked away.

Maddie shut the door and began to get ready. Isabel was sleeping on the bed. She wasn't worried about Jeremy. She'd ditch him as soon as she had the chance. Things were different now. They hadn't been speaking. It was funny, actually. When Jeremy looked at her, when their eyes met across the living room or passing in the hall, it was as if he didn't recognize her, as if he'd forgotten everything that had happened.

Chapter 53

I am wandering in a dark forest of densely packed trees. Moss shifts and settles among the branches like spiderwebs in a light breeze. There is a sound that fills the air like the boom of a passing airplane, a loud and steady groan, deep in pitch, then falling away, then deep again. It is the only sound present because the forest is empty of wildlife, not a single call from a distant bird, or scratching of a squirrel. The sound rises. The sound falls. At its loudest it vibrates in my ears, making it difficult to form coherent thoughts.

After a while, I come upon a small village of shriveled huts, nestled into a clearing at the edge of the forest. I walk to the center of the village and look around. A thin and naked man, the chief, approaches me and speaks, but his words are lost in the rising noise. Then I see the source of the cacophonous booming.

Not far from the village, the forest thins, giving out onto a gray beach and a silver lake. Beached partially in the water and partially out is a giant fish-like thing, eyes closed, sleeping, its snoring the source of the booming noise.

As the Great Fish's snoring subsides, I can hear the chief's voice, "—so hungry. What are we to do? We have angered the Great Jonah and he has allowed our crops to die. We have—" But the rest is drowned in the Great Fish's next rising breath.

"Jonah?" I ask, when next my voice can be heard.

The chief points to the great fish. "What do you think we should do?"

I shrug. "Eat the fish."

The chief seems to consider this for a moment. He cocks his head to the side. Then a wicked gleam enters his eye and he shouts something into the air.

Villagers appear as if from nowhere. They are yelling and screaming. They jab their spears and knives at the sky. They run down the beach, set loose, attacking, without hesitation, the great fish. The Great Fish— the whale— gives up its life without protest, the cacophonous breathing suddenly ceasing, opening the air to the cheering of the villagers.

Remaining next to me, the chief smiles, but it is a sad smile. His voice is like a scream now in deafening silence. "NOW," he says. "FOR THE LAST TIME. WE FEAST."

I watch the villagers as they harvest the flesh, cutting away gleaming chunks, plunging their faces ravenously into the ripe pinkness, blood staining their mouths, splattering their naked and emaciated bodies.

Later, as the sun begins to set and it grows dark and cold—the villagers passed out on the beach as if drunk, as if slaughtered in the great fish's blood—I realize what I have allowed to happen.

Somewhere in the dark, I can hear the chief's voice, now only a dying whisper. "What worth the seventeen layers of the human soul?"

I stand in the pitch dark and hear nothing. I hear not a single animal sound or sign of life. I cannot see. There is only the dark and the cold and the void. The silence itself pushes on me, my body crumpling beneath its weight.

And then I hear the chief's voice again, the faintest of whispers, making a list with the last of his breath…

CHAPTER 54

ZACH

Earlier in the day Zach had had to dig out the *Is this a dream?* card from deep within the pocket of his jeans. The card had become worn and smudged and soft like cloth. He'd looked at the card, then up across the playground. He'd blinked. Mr. M hadn't been there, down by the fence at the edge of the playground. Mr. M was always there. Where had he gone? What other business did he have?

Now, it was Friday night, and, sitting alone in his room, he had to consider his situation. His visions hadn't stopped, recurring repetitively through his mind. His friends were in trouble, he knew. (He already thought of the two women and the man from the basement as his friends, although he'd never met them.) He had to help his friends. He knew if he didn't, terrible things were going to happen to them.

The blonde woman was going to try to kill Harold Klimt by attacking the Upshaw Mansion with a hammer. The young, auburn-haired woman was going to sneak in with the party guests and try to get the man in the basement out. And the man in the basement was so distracted by what he was doing, he didn't know what was really going on. Zach also knew there was no way to get to the man in the basement from the front of the house. If they went through the front, they'd be stopped for sure, and—he didn't know how he knew, but he did—they'd never leave. They had to sneak in from the back. He knew the way. He'd been there before, when he'd seen some strange people in one of the rooms and the man from the basement

(Colin. His name was Colin.) had helped lead him out of the house. The man in the basement didn't mean to be doing the awful things he was doing; he couldn't help it. The man in the basement didn't know any better.

Zach knew both of the women were going to the house tonight, that whatever he was going to do, he had to do it now. If he didn't do something—it was simple—they were going to die.

Mesa Rapids was sinking fast.

CHAPTER 55

I've painted the Great Fish on my mural. I've painted its slaughter. I've painted many things. Something keeps dripping on my head from above, but I'm too focused to care now; I wipe it away and continue. I dream, then awaken and I paint, and then, when my eyes close from utter exhaustion, I dream again from the cold concrete floor before it is time to rise again. Sometimes, I think the only thing that wakes me is my own scream, dragging myself up, the brush still in my hand. Nightmares can mess you up permanently. Some people never come back from that shit. *Whose voice? I'm no longer sure. I no longer care. There is one dream, persistent, a nightmare, which I am still unable to remember upon waking. It is the most horrible dream, a constant roaring in my ears, it is... I remember my mom, after she'd read to me and I'd closed my eyes and she thought I was asleep, lightly stroking my hair, saying what she wanted to say and knew would embarrass me during the daytime, but that I secretly adored, "Beautiful boy...my beautiful boy...shhh...my beautiful boy..." But the nightmare interferes, haunts all seventeen layers of my soul...*

CHAPTER 56

LAUREN

Lauren showered until the hot water became lukewarm, and then until it was cold. She did not want to get out, because she knew, when she did, she'd have to finally face the world. She'd made up her mind, and she was determined, but she was scared. She was scared shitless.

"Okay," she said to herself, and jerked the water off. She pulled the shower curtain aside and grabbed a towel from the rack. She swung the towel over her shoulders and stood there, shivering, feeling the water trickling down her freshly shaved legs. She chuckled to herself, relishing the cold evaporation, inhaling the steam in the air, thinking how ridiculous it was that she'd even bothered to shave considering what she was about to do. What perfect "womanly" habits she had these days—look how society had trained her—considering she was the same person who had refused to shave in college, refused to wear a bra, told her boyfriends with smug satisfaction they could take it or leave it. And, as she recalled, they always took it anyway. She cackled, then shut her mouth when she heard how she sounded.

On the kitchen table, she'd arrayed her supplies. She'd scoured the house, unsure what she was looking for, but collecting anything she found that might be useful. She didn't own a gun, had never felt comfortable with one in the house, although she'd grown up on a ranch and her father owned several, but there was no chance in hell she was driving over to the ranch, and besides she did have quite a collection of high-quality kitchen cutlery, the largest and most menacing of which now sat on the table next to a coil of rope, a flashlight, various batteries, a random assortment of silverware, a yellow pad of paper and some pens, her NYU hoodie slung over a chair, a rubber mallet, a claw hammer, a hacksaw, and various other things, anything that could be even remotely useful.

She'd also unburied her college backpack from the bottom of her closet. She felt a twinge of longing when she held it, as she began to fill it with supplies. Nothing specific, really. Just positive feelings from the happiest days of her life, smiling friends, musty dorm rooms. The backpack's weight felt good on her shoulder. It felt solid. Sane. That was good.

She lifted the hammer, felt its weight in her hand, swung it in front of her. She tried to imagine striking someone with it. What would it feel like?

She heard something. She froze. There was a sound, a sound she had just become consciously aware of, but that she knew had been going on for at least a few minutes. It was faint; that's why she hadn't noticed it at first. A scratching, like fingernails on wood. It was coming from the front door.

She crept across the living room, the hammer held out at her side, the backpack slung over her shoulder. She was ready to go, but she didn't like that scratching sound. She didn't like that sound at all. She moved slowly, so she wouldn't make a noise, so she could put her ear against the door and listen.

From up close, the sound was more defined, crunching and splintering, as if those fingernails had split, rubbing, lubricated, becoming squishy.

She leaned to the side, reaching her hand out to the lacy curtains. She cracked the curtain and looked through the window to the side of the door, expecting... What was she expecting? Nothing, actually. She expected to see nobody there. But that wasn't what she saw.

She stifled a cry.

It was the man from the party, the one with the black eyes, the one who had given her the party invitation to Mr. Klimt's soirée. He was nearly motionless, only his hand moving, reached out like a bear paw, slowly dragging his fingers down the door above the knob.

She jerked away from the window, forcing her breathing to be as quiet as possible. She took a couple of careful steps back.

Hello, Lauren. I want to show you something.

"Fuck this," she said under her breath, and bolted. She ran through the house, heading for the back door. She didn't know why the man with the black eyes scared her so much, but her instinct told her not to mess with him, not like this anyway. He'd been sent by Mr. Klimt to head her off, but she wasn't about to let that happen. She tore through the back door and was outside.

The fresh, cool breeze was a momentary relief, felt good on her cheeks, and then she was running. She ran around the house and shot across the front yard, going for her truck. She knew the man with the black eyes was right there, might be coming after her, but she was fast.

Something dark shifted at the corner of her vision.

She leapt over the flower bed, nearly stumbled in the driveway, caught herself and then her hand was fumbling with the door to the truck.

Show you something.

She tore the door open. She jumped inside. She slammed the door closed, ripped the keys from her pocket, jammed the right one into the keyhole, and started the engine.

Another time then.

She was halfway down the block before she realized the hammer was still clutched in her white-knuckled fingers.

CHAPTER 57

MADDIE

It was as if the parties swelled on Friday nights— from the quiet, introspective, yet constant drinking done indoors, to something less negotiable—becoming too much for the Upshaw Mansion to contain, spilling people out into the yard where the drinks circled, talk was done over-loudly or not at all, and, as midnight descended over them, the dancing commenced, often, for many, until collapse.

This Friday was no different. It was the same as the last time she'd been here, Maddie thought. People were everywhere, in swirling clusters, their clothes somewhat less formal, perhaps, than they'd been before, more worn and ragged, sometimes torn in places, but, as far as she could tell, basically the same sort of people. Maddie's plan, once she got inside, was to break off on her own, and go looking for Colin.

Jeremy led them into the house. "All right. Let's party!" he said, somehow already in possession of drinks, passing one to Maddie.

Maddie took hers and held it, but didn't drink. She watched Jeremy toss his back. She kept glancing uneasily at Jeremy, unsure what to make of him.

While Jeremy was getting another drink, she took her opportunity and zigzagged through the people, her escape quickly swallowed by the crowd. She crossed the room. When she got to the curving stairway that led upward, something told her not to go that way. Colin was downward, somewhere where there would be quiet, no matter how extravagant the party became. Colin was somewhere dimly lit; she could almost picture him there, crouched over his sketchbook, pacing the cold floor.

She turned, going around to the hallway behind the stairs. Somewhere, there would be a way into the basement, a doorway leading to some stairs. She had no idea how she knew he'd be down there, only that it made sense. If she were going to undertake a massive art project, she'd need a permanent escape from all of these people too. She'd need a place dark and quiet.

She opened a door, closed it, and immediately the roaring of the party was muffled and behind her. The hallway before her was empty. She began forward, but had only gone a few feet when she heard the door being opened again. She turned to watch Jeremy step into the hallway, then close the door again.

"Where are you going?" he asked.

"I'm looking for Colin."

"Good. I'll look with you," Jeremy said, walking up to stand beside Maddie.

Maddie put her hand up. Her brow knit suspiciously. "Wait a minute. Why?"

"I want to see my old friend."

Maddie considered Jeremy for a moment. There didn't seem to be any of the old hostility in his eyes, his expression unreadable. She sighed. "I guess it can't hurt."

"Good."

They began to walk. The hallway was straight and long and there were many doors to either side of them.

"Where should we try first?" Maddie asked.

"Go straight," Jeremy said. "All the way to the end of the hall."

Chapter 58
LAUREN

Lauren drove through the rubble in the road. On one street, it looked as if someone had gathered all of the potted plants in town and smashed them on the pavement, dark soil speckled with white spilled in little piles, terra-cotta shards crushed to sand beneath the wheels of her truck. On another street, there were piles of electronic equipment—telephones, DVD players, TVs (from vacuum tube to flat screen), speaker systems, computer towers—but her truck drove over the wreckage with ease. Then there was a fallen branch in the road no one had bothered to remove, and she—glad for her vehicle's four-wheel drive—jostled over it.

When she made the next turn, she slowed. The road was clear, but something caught her eye. Two dogs were sitting alert on the sidewalk, watching her intently. One was a cocker spaniel with drooping eyes and ears. The other was a small white terrier. They sat, side by side, their heads turning to track her progress. As she reached the end of the street, they lifted their heads and, in unison, howled into the air. It was a mournful sound, a warning. And then she was headed down the next street.

She could see the Upshaw Mansion now. The sky was already growing dark and there were lights glowing in the windows. There were cars lining the streets, parked bumper to bumper on either side. What day was it? Friday? Damn. The house would be swarming with people. But that didn't matter. Not really.

She parked the truck down the street and got out. She was still holding the hammer, quite liked the feel of it now that she was used to it. She walked up the sidewalk, the backpack firmly strapped over her shoulder.

No one paid any attention to her as she began to cross the yard and thread through the milling people. No one seemed concerned with the hammer in her hand or the look in her eyes. She made it easily into the house.

In the front hall, she began to ask people if they'd seen Mr. Klimt. She was met with shrugs and dismissive nods. She asked a man in a top hat who raised his nose and turned away. A woman in a yellow dress giggled and brought her pale green drink to her lips before she was pulled away into the crowd. No one seemed to really be seeing her. They shook their heads, said things like, "I'm afraid not," and then their attentions were drawn elsewhere, as if she were of little importance, no threat at all.

By the time the current of the crowd dumped her on the other side of the room, she was beginning to wonder what it was she had been planning to do exactly. Her boyfriend had spent the entire evening last time looking all over the house for Mr. Klimt and never found him. How was she going to?

Her boyfriend...Mark... Loneliness washed through her, helplessness; she hated that ineffectual feeling more than anything else.

There was a lone chair against the wall. She sat, letting the hammer rest on her knees. There were terrible things going on; she had to remember that. People were blinded by the parties, by the extravagance, by the strange horrors. They were ignoring the problem. She knew Harold Klimt was responsible. He'd lured nearly the entire town into his house and hypnotized them somehow, pacified them. If she killed him, if she bashed his brains in with her hammer, she believed, it would all go away. It was an illusion, everything she'd seen. If she destroyed the man responsible, she'd wake up from this horrible nightmare. She could picture the swinging hammer now, connecting metal against bone, crunching wetly, reverberating through her arm. She ran her hands through her hair, wiped her lips with the back of her wrist. In the corner, there was a small table, set with a tray of drinks and a lamp.

She stood, approached the table. She looked behind her, glancing over her shoulders. No one was paying any attention. Nobody was even looking her way.

She reached out, and swept the tray of drinks from the table, where they shattered on the floor, the metal tray clattering loudly. She threw her backpack to the floor, raised the hammer up over her head, and brought it down on the lamp; it crunched solidly. She kicked the table on its side. She turned, looking for more, saw a painting on the wall, swung the hammer, tore the canvas, splintered the frame. Then she attacked the chair she'd just been sitting on only moments before, smashing through the seat, toppling, smashing and smashing.

She looked up. She'd gotten their attention. People from the crowd had turned to watch her, their mouths closing, conversations ceased.

Perhaps, she thought wildly, she could get Klimt to come to her.

She leapt toward the next things she saw: a chaise lounge; something framed behind glass in a box hanging above it; a figural sculpture tying the three objects together. "Move," she said to the sitting couple, who stood and backed away to either side, watching her intently. She kicked one of the wooden legs free and buried her hammer in the cotton padding, getting the claw stuck in the springs. She wrenched the hammer free and lifted it. Could she really ruin the sculpture before her? Hadn't she devoted her life to the pursuit and celebration of the artistic? Hadn't she always considered herself to have more reverence and respect for the creative process than most? The hammer came down. The sculpture's face disintegrated, shards of ceramic shooting every which way; she felt one zing her cheek, but she was beyond caring. There was something in the back of her mind, words spooling through her head. She kicked the sculpture; it thumped to the floor. She crushed its abdomen, then jumped up and swung the hammer to the side, striking the box on the wall, sending it flying, shattering. She stomped her foot. Inside there was a feather and a note: "da Vinci's Quill."

Bullshit. It was all bullshit. She crushed that too, felt it snap beneath her foot. She was vaguely aware of a sound escaping her, heard it as if from a distance, her cackling laughter.

Art doesn't matter without life, Mark had said to her once through that cocky smile of his. And he was right. Besides, they were all fakes—everything she'd seen. These were not priceless artifacts. They were bullshit.

Art doesn't matter without life…art doesn't…life…

She swung around, continuing to laugh like a crazy person, looking for more things to smash with her hammer. She froze, the hammer raised.

The first thing she became aware of was their eyes: empty. They had fallen silent, everyone in the crowd, all of them. They were *all* looking at *her.*

Then she saw their grins, huge, maniacal. Calmly, they began to close in.

Lauren brought the hammer up, defensively this time. She was confused. She was trembling. She was scared. But she didn't scream. Not, that is, until their grins began to widen and widen, segmenting their faces, splitting, like cleaved fruit, their heads opened and gaping and greasy.

Then she screamed.

Chapter 59

The Seventeen Layers of the Human Soul:

The hypnagogic state
Astral extremities
Mental projection
Mathematics
Rain
The ethereal wall
The odor of wind
Sex
Walking as if on water
The twenty-seven colors of the Umbra Ina
Otherworldly emissions
History
Purple membrane
Muck
The memory of trees
Red
Roaring in the ears

I'm troubled I may be losing myself in this basement. All sense of time has slipped. It could be hours or days, gone. Flipping through the pages of this journal, there's so much here I don't remember writing. It's my handwriting, all of it, ravings, perhaps most disturbing some moments for which I have no recognition. And others I remember transcribing, which seem to be missing.

No one else is down here. No other hands could have touched this journal, but… It's odd. There are jagged marks, in the spine, where pages have been torn free. One torn in half. An entire section missing. Why? Where are these pages? I've scoured the piles of papers I've sorted from the boxes, thinking I may have added my own pages to one of them, but they're all mixed up now. I've lost track of everything.

I awoke, and immediately began to write down The Nightmare— *the one that awakens me with my own screams—before I could forget it. But now it's gone. Pages lost. I can't remember, yet it haunts me. That terrible roaring sound approaching, closer and closer…*

Nightmares can mess you up permanently.

The mural is almost finished, I think. I've dreamed of creatures and I've painted them. They swirl and cavort, and people speak with them or are torn apart. I've put everything I have into this mural— my mural, my masterpiece. The great tournament swirl of human emotions I've flung into my work. I've screamed and cried, been joyful, and then crushed that joy, for in human joy is ignorance, blind we are to the black truth. These dancing demons.

It was Gar, his puffy, reddened face peeking over my shoulder, when all I wanted was to leave the basement, feeling suffocated, pounding furiously on the locked door, losing control, slinging paint in angry swathes. It was Fel, blank and white like fog, when I became too exhausted to remain awake and, for a time, drifted into sleep, dreamless, however brief. It was Glan as I rose up and looked at what I'd done, heart beating warmly in my chest, and was proud. It was Ulk when Maddie smiled tentatively from the darkness of my mind, and she giggled mischievously and turned away, and I hung my head, eyes stinging with tears. And Cilia as I masturbated miserably into an old cloth. And Mar when the veil fell over me, wrapped my trembling self, bore me up, and I no longer cared.

I've lost sense of what's real and what's not. I paint. The light is dim and never changes. Sometimes I sleep in the recliner and sometimes on the floor. There are plain sandwiches in a small refrigerator under the stairs and I eat those when I'm hungry, drink water from unlabeled glass bottles when I'm thirsty.

Some people never come back from this shit.

I wish I could go to Elephant House. I wish I could confess to Donnie my troubles. He'd help me stay true, stay levelheaded, rational. He'd recommend, with a grin and a wave, a one night stand with an LLL, a Lovely-Lonely-Lady. And right now, I'd be happy for such an experience, to touch someone, feel her blood pumping beneath her skin, share her warmth, lick her sweat, her sex. Did any of that even happen? Any of my strange and vulgar encounters? I'm no longer sure which parts I made up and which are actually true. Either way, afterward, I'm empty.

What worth the human soul? What use?

Wait! I think I remember! Horrible, truly horrible! In The Nightmare, *I am not myself. It's an unsettling feeling. I am*

CHAPTER 60

[Missing Pages]

CHAPTER 61
MESA RAPIDS

A nd in the street, a manhole cover shuddered, and blood seeped up in a circle.

And Chelsea stayed home from school to prepare for the event to which she'd invited all of her friends: a "knife party."

And Cleveland Clovis, an elderly and respected architect—responsible for the unconventional layout and appearance of city hall and the public library in Mesa Rapids—had been having lots of bad dreams. He hadn't left his house in a week. He'd slept, when he had to, in his bed. And when one of his nightmares—jagged and red—was finally so terrifying his heart could no longer take it, and he awoke gasping for breath and with pain shooting down his arm, his house circled by dogs, their heads lifted and howling mournfully.

And Zach saw the people begin to dance and heard the screams.

And many people saw characters from the television show, *Meet the Newmans*, walking around (they lived in a house down Carpenter Street on The Hill). The pilot show had premiered on NBC last Sunday and everyone in town had watched it. Sometimes the Newmans were seen together, talking quietly among themselves, as if conspiring—Harvey, the father, wearing a spacesuit.

And Rich, who had given up his room to Colin so he could work for his dad in Denver, and hated his new job, wanted more than anything to move back to the place with his friends. But that was the problem, wasn't it? Go back to—where? He couldn't remember the name of the place. In fact, he couldn't even remember what it looked like, or the faces of his friends. It was as if the place had erased itself from the memory of the outside world. And when he said "fuck it," and tried to drive out there for a visit, he got lost in the woods around Blue Bear Lake. He ran out of gas and he walked, and when he crested the hill, he saw the lake of blood, the ocean of blood, spreading to the horizon, reflected in the clouds, filling his vision until his eyes hurt, bubbling in places, steaming. He stared, until his legs gave out, and he collapsed.

And Allen Munroe followed his brother out of the nameless bar and across the street and into the woods. He stepped along the path and came into a small clearing, could hear the babbling of nearby water. He stopped and his brother beckoned him to follow. "No," he said, shaking his head, thinking of his son Zach. When his brother attacked him, he strangled him and dumped his body in the river.

And Les and Cass had been wandering the halls of the Upshaw Mansion for a long time. They didn't know how long. Hours? Days? Weeks? When they were too tired to go on, they found an empty room and slumped to the floor. The door slowly closed itself after them. When Les looked over at her friend, Cass was already sleeping. She felt warm. Water lapped against her. She was lying in the sand on the beach. She could hardly feel the water because she and it were nearly the same temperature. It covered her legs and rose up over her body. The room filled with blood.

And Detective Reynolds was seen skipping down the street hand in hand with his dead wife.

And in Colin's old room at the house something stirred. The bird, at the center of Colin's sculpture, roused by whatever forces swam in the air about Mesa Rapids, began to flutter and beat.

And the mural in the basement of the Upshaw Mansion was nearly complete.

CHAPTER 62

ZACH

As much as Zach preferred not to step on the shriveled baby heads, didn't like the sliding squish beneath his sneakers, he was in a hurry and there were too many of them, actually apples, fallen and rotting from the trees in the unkempt garden behind the Upshaw Mansion.

When he came to the empty and overgrown swimming pool, he stopped. The bushes on the other side had grown large, covered in ivy, snaking down to reach out over the moss-covered muck at the bottom of the pool, now little more than an indent, like an open grave for a large animal. He knew he shouldn't linger, that the blonde woman was in trouble and she needed help, but there was something significant about this spot, something he didn't understand.

A revelation tingled at the back of his mind like an itch, but he didn't have time to ponder it, and when something bubbled noisily from the far corner of the swimming pool, he forgot everything and hurried on, beginning to run.

A branch whipped at his face, but he didn't care and batted it away with one arm. He had no idea what he was doing; he was running purely on instinct. He was scared, but that was okay. His dad wouldn't miss him, if something bad happened. What did it matter? His best friend was dead, his friend's parents dead. Kids in his class were dead. His teacher had gone missing yesterday, probably dead. Was it not better to run into the mouth of the beast to get it over with than to hide and have to live in constant fear, knowing it was only a matter of time before he was found and torn to shreds?

But that's not really how you feel, is it?

Whose voice was that? His mother's? Maybe, but he didn't think so. He couldn't remember his mother's voice. She'd been gone from his life for too long, died when he was young. He didn't even miss her, not really. Sometimes he missed the idea of a mother, but he'd learned to be independent. He'd had to. It was no big deal.

It's up to you now.

And he knew that was true. It was time to fight back. He'd been scared for too long. Mr. M had been watching him, to see what he'd do, and he'd done nothing. He was just a kid, after all. But he knew now that was only an excuse. He'd seen what his dad became when he was on one of his drunken benders. Adults could be as childish as kids. And he could act and make a difference if he wanted to. Everyone in Mesa Rapids had become a victim. It was time he did something about it.

He slowed as he came up to the walls of the mansion. He knew where there was a back door and he found it easily. There were three concrete steps leading up to it and on the second step he had a moment of panic; he clutched himself as his heart beat wildly, digging his trembling hands into his pockets. It's not there. Oh, god. You've lost it. But there it was. His fingers slid the battered, cloth-like card from his pocket. *Is this a dream?* Well, we're about to find out, he thought, and forced his legs to lift and pump beneath him, opening the door, stepping inside.

He was in a small entryway room and then the hallway stretched on and on to his right and to his left. He'd taken no more than a couple of steps when the door behind him clicked closed, not slamming, just closing quietly, confidently; amused. It was a subtle sound, but it still made him cringe. He took a deep breath, and turned to the right.

At the first door, he stopped. He wanted to test his theory, but first he checked his supplies. He had a flashlight filled with fresh batteries clipped to his belt, the pocketknife his uncle had given him tucked into his back pocket, a silver lighter, the card the man from the basement had given him, and a plain red bandana he'd rolled up and tied around his forehead to keep his shaggy hair out of his eyes like a character from an anime cartoon. He opened the door.

He stood in the doorway and tried to control his breathing. The room was empty except for an old man sitting crouched forward on a lone chair. The old man had a knife in one hand and his index finger extended with the other; he was slowly whittling his finger with the knife, taking thin curls of flesh with each swipe. Below him, to catch the shavings and the blood, there was a tin bucket. Blood dripped from the old man's finger.

Plink...plink...

"'Ello, young feller," the old man said, and continued to whittle.

Plink.

Zach held the card up so he could read it: *Is this a dream?*

He looked at the old man. The old man did *not* disappear.

Plink.

Slowly, he closed the door. His heart felt like a bird trapped in his throat, fighting to get out. He swallowed and forced his breathing to slow. So now he knew. These things he saw were not dreams; they were not visions. They were real, at least for him. And they could probably hurt him if they wanted to. *Don't worry. You have more control than you know.*

Now hurry. Go to the front ballroom at the end of the hallway. Go!

In his mind he could see the blonde woman's face smeared with terror, clawing hands, blood. He began to run.

CHAPTER 64

LAUREN

Lauren swung the hammer in a wide arc. "Get back. Get away from me." She could hear the fear in her voice, the panic. She swung the hammer fast, wishing it would make a whistling sound as it parted the air, but she knew it was too heavy.

Their hands reached out as they came closer, gurgling, no longer capable of words.

"No! Please!" The first hand that came close enough, she struck with the hammer. She expected it to make a dull thumping sound, but instead it was like a baseball striking a bat—*crack*. And the hand flung away, but the horde was unconcerned. More hands reached out for her.

Some of them were making bubbling, *glurging* sounds, that might have been laughter.

The hands twisted and flexed and came together in a writhing mass as they closed in. She swung the hammer wildly, striking many of them, but to no effect. She shattered one hand and another came to fill its place. She screamed, yet part of her couldn't believe her situation—refused to accept it—was calm and reasonable in her head. *Don't worry. This will be over soon. It's not really happening, anyway, but if it is, it will be over soon.*

"No! No!"

And then she noticed certain faces in the crowd. Not everyone's head had split open. Some looked confused, pulled along with the crowd.

One man was very close, looking right at her without any

sign of menace in his eyes, his hands out and flexing because everyone else was doing it.

"Please," Lauren shouted to the man. "Stop them."

A funny look came into the man's eyes as he glanced from side to side, as if finally seeing the split-open heads, the yawning grins filled with blood, horror filling his face. Then he shook his head dismissively, unable to accept such terror.

One of the hands grabbed Lauren's blouse, pulling her into the mob. Another wrapped itself in her hair, tugging painfully. She was no longer screaming, resigned to her fate. Another hand caught her wrist, shook, but her grip refused to let the hammer fall. Hands groped over her body, tearing her clothes, grabbing her breasts. "No," she said to herself, without conviction. The hands were scratching her now, ripping at her flesh. She closed her eyes and waited to be torn apart.

"Wait," someone shouted. It might have been the man who'd been looking at her without menace. "Don't you see what's going on?"

For a moment, the hands hesitated, frozen in whatever horrible and humiliating thing they were doing.

Lauren looked up, through the canopy of limbs and bodies, and could make out the man's face, smiling and triumphant.

"It's a game," the man shouted, raised his glass, and smashed it into the face of the woman standing next to him.

The crowd began to roar. Bodies surged and twisted. People shouted. "A game! A game!"

From her position crouched on the floor, Lauren couln't see much, but she knew a fight had broken out. She could hear people hitting other people, things smashing, maniacal laughing. Many of the hands fell away, turning to defend the bodies that held them. Others, her conviction renewed, she fought off, kicking and thrashing. The hand dropped from her wrist and she swung the hammer back and forth until it was free. She lifted it high, and brought it down on the forearm of the hand clutching her ankle, a sound like snapping plastic. She struggled to her feet, the hammer flew, buried itself in the neck of one of the head-split people. She wrenched it free, blood pumping. It was her turn to laugh, a crazy laugh.

More came at her, swiping at her face, clawing at her eyes, looking for vulnerable soft spots. She fought them off as best she could. At least she was on her feet again. One hand wrenched at her side, scraping skin and flesh. Another got a hold of her hair again and ripped a large wad from her head. She laughed, the hammer breaking another hand, but she couldn't win. There were too many. At least she'd go out smiling.

"Lady," someone was shouting. "Hurry!"

She was backed into the corner now, where the table with the lamp and drinks had been before she'd knocked it over.

"Lady, please."

The claw end of the hammer sunk into the chest of one of them, satisfying, tearing it free.

"Hurry. Come on."

The voice was coming from behind her. She glanced over her shoulder and there was a full-sized door she hadn't noticed before. Peeking from around the partial opening was a boy.

Without much thought, Lauren dived for the door. The boy opened it enough for her to squeeze through and then tried to slam it closed, but a forearm was in the way, a groping hand tearing at the air. Lauren brought the hammer down. The wrist broke easily, clumping sideways, and then she flung the door closed with the full force of her body.

Lauren sunk to the floor with her back against the door. She let her hammer-wielding hand fall to the floor. She fought to catch her breath.

"You, uh…" the boy said.

Lauren held up her hand. "One minute."

The boy was staring at her. "You might want to…"

Lauren looked down at herself. Her clothes were torn and stained with blood, her blouse ripped and open. She looked up and saw where they boy was looking. She began to laugh.

The boy smiled a little, unsure what he should do. Lauren laughed even harder as she fumbled to tie her blouse in a knot about her midriff. She laughed so hard she couldn't sit up and rolled over on the floor. When she'd recovered enough to look up again, she saw that the boy was laughing too, tears streaming down his face.

Chapter 65

COLIN

Colin licked and chewed on his lip, licked it again. He'd been painting for a long time now. He could see it finally. He painted in a feverish haze, unmindful of the drip from above. He was using a large brush now, and thick paint, slapping it on, working furiously, his arm aching, but he didn't care. He was almost finished. The project was nearly complete.

He dipped the brush in the paint, brought it up, as if in slow motion, and wiped it over the wall. He was perched at the top of the step ladder he'd found while digging around in the basement. His tongue flicked out, ran over the roughness of his lips, he chewed, nearly breaking the skin. Something dripped in his hair. He hadn't slept well in a long time, but he now felt perfectly awake, in a jagged, humming consciousness.

A creaking sound made his head shake, but didn't break his concentration. Light entered the basement.

"Good evening, my friend," a familiar voice said.

He didn't let it stop him, dipped the brush, continued to paint.

"By all means, don't stop on my account. I only wanted to watch the final moments. You don't mind, do you?"

The stairs creaked.

"Good. Oh, good. You finally understand," Harold Klimt said, clearly pleased.

Colin grinned, painted and painted. He dipped his brush in the bucket of red, painted over everything. He painted over the creature in the glass chamber. He painted over the Great Fish.

He painted over all those demons and all those tortured people. He dipped his brush, filled the wall until it smeared and ran down in streaks.

Klimt laughed and began to dance a little.

Blood trickled down from above.

Chapter 66
MADDIE

"You're going to want to see this," Jeremy said.

Maddie was nervous, something wasn't right.

"See what?"

"Here. This door. Always at the end of the hall."

They stopped before a door, set into the wall at the end of the hallway. It felt as if they'd been walking forever.

"Go ahead," Jeremy said. "Open it."

Maddie reached out her hand, touched the knob. It was cold. She hesitated. She looked at Jeremy.

(*His eyes are different. What's wrong with his eyes?*)

She turned the knob and opened the door.

At first, she couldn't see anything. It was too dark. And then a strange smell assaulted her, acrid, metallic. She took a step back, then saw a small platform and then wooden stairs leading down. The walls were concrete, she could see that much. Colin was here; she knew it.

Tentatively, she stepped through the doorway and into the basement. She could feel Jeremy following behind her.

She came to the balcony and looked over the side. The first thing that caught her eye was the mural; it was huge, covered the entire wall. And it was intricate, filled with detail, people twisted together, wailing faces, strange creatures. Then she saw Colin, painting red over the entire thing, about halfway across; and a man with immaculately oiled hair, sport coat, and shiny shoes, who had to be Mr. Klimt, standing behind Colin, watching him work, nodding his head in constant approval.

"Colin," she called to him.

Mr. Klimt snapped his head up. "What are you doing here?"

"Colin! Hey! Colin!"

Slowly, continuing to move the brush up and down, Colin lifted his head. "Mm…Maddie?"

Maddie rushed down the stairs. She veered around Mr. Klimt, who stepped forward to stop her, and embraced Colin forcefully. She clutched him so tightly it knocked the brush out his hand, slapping the floor. "Oh, Colin. I missed you. Are you all right? Things are fucked. I'm so glad you're okay. You're okay, right?"

Slowly, Colin brought his hands up and hugged her back. "Maddie? Maddie?"

Too choked up to speak, Maddie could only grip him tighter.

"All right," Mr. Klimt said. "That's quite enough. He only has a little more to do. Let him finish."

Reluctantly, Maddie let go of Colin. She looked at him. He looked haggard and aged. "What's in your hair?"

"Yes. All right," Mr. Klimt said, coming forward, grabbing Maddie's arm and pulling her away.

Maddie looked at the paint bucket, then up at the mural. "What's in your hair, Colin? What is that?"

Colin brought his hand up, touched his head. His fingers came away red. He looked up. He sniffed his fingers, shrugged.

Maddie shook her head forcefully, Mr. Klimt holding her back by her arms. "Blood! It's blood!"

"I don't underst—"

"That's enough of that," Mr. Klimt said.

Maddie broke free and came forward, but someone else caught her, spun her around. It was Jeremy. She struggled to free her hands, but his grip was vise-like, inhuman. He grinned at her, grabbed her hair and yanked. She cried out, and then she saw the knife, pressed against her throat, she could even read the words embossed in its wooden handle: *Meet the Newmans!*

Colin stood, his face painted with misery. "Wait…"

"All right then. Excellent," Mr. Klimt said. "Now finish what you started." Colin took a step forward.

Jeremy pulled Maddie's head back, pressing the knife into

her soft flesh. "I don't think so."

Colin stopped. "Let her go, Jeremy."

Jeremy grinned. "Jeremy? Did I tell you my name was Jeremy? I was lying. I'm Derek. You remember me, don't you, stupid fuck?"

Maddie watched Colin's face pale, fill with terror. It was as if he'd been slapped, as if his worst suspicions had been confirmed. Visibly shaking, he turned, lifted the brush, dunked it in the bucket of blood, and began once more to paint.

Chapter 67 ☐ Zach

"Who are you?" the blonde woman asked him, still slumped on the floor, trying to catch her breath.

Zach stood shyly, shifting his weight from one foot to the other. "I'm Zach."

The woman smiled. "Nice to meet you, Zach. I'm Lauren. What are you doing here?"

"I came to save you."

Lauren began to laugh, but then stopped herself when she saw Zach was serious. She looked at Zach closely. "Well, I guess you did then. Thank you."

Zach dropped his eyes to the floor. "You're welcome. We should probably go."

"Go? Go where?"

"The others. We have to stop the man in the basement."

Lauren scowled. "Klimt? You mean Harold Klimt? Do you know where he is?"

"He's there too," Zach said. "He's making the man do something horrible, something he can't take back when he's done."

"Who is? I don't know what you're talking about, kid."

Zach could feel their time running out, but he struggled with what to say. "He gave me this," he said, fishing the card from his pocket.

Lauren took the card from Zach's outreached hand. She looked at it. "What's this supposed to mean?"

Zach shifted his weight back and forth, back and forth. "It means this is all really happening."

Lauren looked at Zach without comprehension. "It means,"

Zach tried again, "we're not dreaming or imagining any of this stuff." He waved his hands around vaguely. "And you're one of the only ones who can see Mr. M like I do."

"Mr. M?"

"The man with the black eyes."

(Call me Mr. M.)

Zach could see a shudder run through Lauren, and the recognition in her eyes. She knew who he was talking about.

Lauren was still looking at him with an intensity that made him uncomfortable. "We have to go," Zach said.

Lauren sighed. "Okay," she said. She began to lift herself. "But you said Harold Klimt was there, right?"

"Yes. He's there."

Lauren smirked. "Good. I have to kill him."

Zach blinked. "But that's not—"

Something thumped the door—loud enough to cause the hinges to rattle and the wood to groan, echoing down the hallway—and both Zach and Lauren jumped. Zach stepped forward to help Lauren up, but she waved him away. Lauren lifted herself. "Shit," she said. "I haven't felt this beat up since the time I tried Bikram yoga."

The door thumped again.

"Are they trying to get through?" Zach could hear the fear in his voice, but hoped Lauren couldn't.

"Sounds like it."

"We have to go."

"Door seems solid. I wouldn't worry about it." But she raised her hammer.

Zach's heart was caught in his throat as they waited for the next thump. They waited for several minutes, but it didn't come.

"See," Lauren said. "Nothing to—"

The wood groaned. It was suddenly hot in the hallway, the air thick with moisture.

As if the crack beneath the door were a throat that had been cut, blood began to pulse out over the floor. It rushed at their feet, dark and steaming, fresh.

"What the fuck?" Lauren said.

Zach tugged at Lauren's arm. "Come on. Come on."

Blood was pumping from beneath all of the doors in the hallway. It had already filled the open spaces, began to creep up their shoes.

"All right," Lauren said. "Let's go. Go!"

Zach took Lauren's hand and they ran down the hall, splashing in the blood; then slogging through it as it came up to their ankles, and then their knees.

They struggled forward. They had to get to the end of the hall. There was a door there (if it wasn't filled with blood) that led to the basement. But there was an image in Zach's head, an image of blood erupting from the ground and creeping over the landscape—of an ocean, molten and putrid—and a nagging voice in Zach's head told him it was already too late.

Chapter 68

COLIN

"Colin. Please," Maddie said.

Colin flinched.

"If you stop, I'll cut her throat," Jeremy/Derek said.

"That's right," Klimt said. "More blood."

Colin continued to paint. He felt trapped inside a bad dream, raging with fever. But he was nearly done now; it would all be over soon and he could go home.

"You have to stop," Maddie said.

Colin glanced over his shoulder. Jeremy/Derek held the point of the knife so that it actually indented the soft skin on Maddie's neck, drawing a thin smear of blood. Mr. Klimt was standing next to them, watching him intently, his eyes excited. Behind them, however, which caught his longing gaze despite the horror of his situation, there was a small window that looked out through a window well, letting faint moonlight in, contrasting in a muddy mix with the dull and naked bulbs that hung from the ceiling.

From above came faint thumping sounds and groaning wood. It had become hot in the basement. He wiped sweat from his forehead and turned back to his mural. His mind was dull, too tired to cope. All he could do was drop the brush in the bucket, bring it up, and sop it over everything.

"I wish I myself could have been the one to finish." Klimt sighed. "At least I'll see it done. No one before me can say that."

"You don't know what you're doing," Maddie said. "Mesa Rapids has become—"

"A nightmare?" Jeremy/Derek offered. "Great, isn't it? One wild fucking party."

"Yes," Klimt said. "A party. Like no other."

Chapter 69
THE BIRD

Most had left their homes and now wandered the streets like war victims, shell-shocked, staring blankly at the things they saw, careful to veer around the largest and deepest puddles of blood, so that when they caught a glimpse of the construct shambling down the sidewalk, their minds were unable to translate what it was they were seeing into definable terms. It was made from all manner of materials: fractured bits of furniture, glass, machine parts, held together with wire and fused by heat. It had a face, people supposed, but the expressions it made were difficult to gaze upon. It wasn't that they were frightening, but that they were expressions representative of emotions beyond human understanding. At its center, something struggled, as if caught in an intricate frame of wires, a bird trapped, fluttering frantically like the panicked beating of a heart. It moved slowly but steadily toward the Upshaw Mansion.

Chapter 70

LAUREN

When the blood was more than a couple of feet deep, they were forced to swim, and the ceiling grew closer and closer to smothering them. Zach, Lauren could see, was not a good swimmer, and thrashed along, quickly tiring. She, however, was an excellent swimmer and helped Zach as best she could.

Lauren kept her head down and refused to panic. She refused to die. She'd averted death already once today and now she felt she had to do it again. She also had to save Zach. He was special somehow and she knew she needed him for something. They all needed him, everyone remaining in Mesa Rapids. He seemed to be the only one who actually knew what was going on. She prayed he also knew how to stop it.

She could see the end of the hallway now and, just as Zach had promised, there was a door, but the blood had risen nearly to its top. She desperately hoped it opened inward.

Zach sputtered in the blood, flailing, sinking, pushing his face up desperately to stay above the surface. It wasn't like swimming in water, it was thicker, stickier; cloying. The smell was nauseating. She'd watched Zach vomit while they'd still been on their feet, pale and chunky. It was viscous like soup and warm, just the right temperature to lull the muscles in the body to relax. She helped the boy, lifting him beneath his arms until he could hook his fingers over the quarter-inch door frame, barely enough to keep him afloat.

They had maybe twelve inches of space remaining. And less

and less with each minute that passed. She had to get the door open. She dived, but the blood was too thick for her to open her eyes. She groped her hands out blindly for the doorknob. The blood was difficult to push through. She surfaced, afraid of losing her bearings.

Zach's clinging fingers were now below the surface of the blood, his face beginning to turn upward, his head connecting with the ceiling. "Open it," the boy said to her. "Please open it."

She dived. She didn't have a choice. Her nails scraped painfully on the wood. She found the doorknob, grasped and pulled. She could feel her feet completely submerging in the sticky warmth.

The doorknob wouldn't turn. She tried to turn it. Jammed.

She needed air, flailing, pumping her arms to the surface. For a moment, it seemed too far away; the blood must have reached the ceiling. But then she came up into inches of air, pushing her face into the ceiling, gasping.

She didn't have time to check for the boy. She dived. This was her last chance. She took the doorknob in both hands and yanked. Nothing happened.

No. Be calm, she told herself.

She forced herself to relax. Her lungs ached for air. She turned the doorknob.

CHAPTER 71

COLIN

A woman's face screamed at him as he slapped blood over her features, silencing her, drowning her out. He was almost done. He had only the top left corner and then his mural would be complete. For that, he'd need the ladder.

Slowly, Colin walked over to the ladder and began to drag it over to where he needed it to be. He glanced over to make sure Maddie was still okay. Jeremy/Derek still had the knife at her throat; Maddie had fallen silent.

"I guess I should have asked this a long time ago. *What* are you exactly?" he said to Mr. Klimt.

Klimt chuckled. "I'm just a man, like you. And like you, I was given an opportunity. Someone very interesting came to me, named me his associate, but my family—"

"Yeah, yeah," Jeremy/Derek interjected. "Your family got in the way. Blah, blah, everyone dies. We've heard it all before, old man. Let my friend finish for fuck's sake."

Colin lifted the bucket and began to climb the ladder. He set the bucket on the platform provided for such a task, grabbed the brush, and began to paint over the last of the Great Fish, its large eye awake and accusing through the lazy folds of its flesh. "What's going to happen when I finish here?"

"Freedom," Klimt said. "What do you mean by—"

"Just shut up and finish the damn thing already," Jeremy/Derek said.

Colin dunked the brush, lifted it, painted.

"You have to stop," Maddie said, almost a whisper. "You can't worry about me."

"Shut up, bitch," Jeremy/Derek said.

Colin froze, the brush suspended in the air, dripping thick strands of crimson. Maddie was right. Something was wrong, and just because he couldn't understand it, did not mean it wasn't a threat. "Who was this interesting person, the one who gave you the job?" he asked, bringing the brush up but not applying it to the wall this time, stalling.

"Oh, that's right, I don't believe you've ever met him. He—"

"I have," Jeremy/Derek interrupted again. "He's quite a character. You're gonna fucking love him, Colin. Just wait."

Colin turned his head so he could look down at Jeremy/Derek. "I want to hear Mr. Klimt tell his story, asshole."

Jeremy/Derek bristled, pointing the knife at him, his other hand still firmly gripping Maddie's hair. "You were always such a pussy. You think too much, Colin. You have a job to do, now get it done or I'm going to cut your girlfriend open and see what's inside her, fuck her while she's still warm." He whipped the knife back to Maddie's throat.

Colin could feel his face growing hot. He could feel the emotion rising up in him, finally. It was anger and it was hate, but it was also feelings true and raw. He'd stewed in depression and self-loathing for too long. The anger felt good. The hate felt very good. "When this is done, I'm going to cut your fucking head off, Derek."

Jeremy/Derek jumped, for a moment surprised by these words of backlash. Then he smiled. "When this is done, there'll be more blood to spill than just yours and this pretty little thing," he said, dry-humping Maddie from behind, exaggerating, making disgusting pig sounds.

Colin stood upright on the ladder, angry but also relishing his pumping heart. He held out the crimson-dripping brush like a weapon.

Jeremy/Derek thrust himself into Maddie's backside.

Maddie suppressed a whimper. "Colin…don't…"

"But that's just it, isn't it?" Klimt broke in suddenly, as if still following an earlier train of thought. "You asked what I am. What am I—what are all of us—but walking wads of flesh? Pierce us, even a little, and we bleed out our lives in the dirt…"

That's when the door burst open and blood like a raging storm crashed into the basement.

CHAPTER 72

ZACH

It's like being inside a seashell, Zach thought.

He could hardly feel his body, wrapped in warm liquid, buoyed up, flung forward and down. He was aware he was moving, drawn on by the rushing current. And it was loud. He could taste it in his mouth, inhaled through his nose and swallowed, thick and rusty, sliding down his throat. And it was in his eyes, the world tinted red. He was inside a shell, inside the sea, spun round and round the nautiloid spiral.

He dipped below the surface; it was at the surface he could feel it most. Then, below, it was the same temperature as his skin, floating nowhere. Until he opened his eyes and it burned red, felt as if his eyeballs were melting away. And his chest raged and he couldn't help himself, inhaling the blood into his lungs. Killing him. The black spots killing him as they closed in.

Then the surface again, peeling away at him, coughing up blood that wasn't his. Crying out for air. Cold. Suddenly cold. Trembling. He could feel his arms again, his hands wiping at his face, clawing the blood from the crevasses about his eyes. His eyes watered furiously, faint signs of the world now tinted pink as he thrashed around. For some reason he could feel his hair, like a wool helmet glued over his head. He was on his hands and knees in several inches of pooled blood, vomiting, retching in horror and disgust.

Slowly, he began to make out his surroundings. It was dim. "Lauren? Lauren?"

"I'm here."

"Die. Piece of shit."

"Wads of flesh? The human soul?"

"Lauren?"

And then she had him by the shoulders. She hugged him tight. "It's okay, kid. It's okay."

The blood thrashed, sounds of a struggle. The man from the basement, Colin, was grappling with someone; he had his hands around the other person's throat. Colin squeezed, cords on his neck bulging, his face streaming blood. The man beneath him struggled, clawing at Colin's face, desperately kicking, pushed beneath the surface of the blood. Colin's eyes were wild, bright through his crimson mask. He held on until the man beneath him stopped moving, legs still, arms sinking, the surface tranquil, filming, a lone fly alighting, buzzing away.

Colin remained kneeling, his chest heaving. The young woman with the auburn hair from his dreams sloshed up behind Colin. Colin leaned back and the woman clutched him to her belly, hugging his head tightly.

"You're here," Zach said.

Colin and the young woman with the auburn hair looked up at him.

"What are your names?" Zach asked.

"I'm Maddie," the woman said. "And this is Colin."

Zach rushed forward, floundering in the blood. He threw one arm around Maddie's waist and the other around Colin's shoulders. His eyes continued to sting with tears.

Maddie looked down on him, astonished. "Oh," she said, then brought her hand out to pat his back.

Colin blinked at him.

"I've found you," Zach said.

Lauren walked up to them. "Lauren," she said, extending her hand, then drawing it back when she saw how they were arranged, nodded her head. "It's good to meet you."

Something else thrashed in the blood. All four of their heads snapped up and turned. Mr. Klimt was moving toward the stairs, but he was having a hard time negotiating through the blood. When he saw them looking, he leapt forward, his face a bloodstained mask of panic.

"I don't think so," Lauren said, and stomped around their huddled group. She moved easily, resolutely. She still, somehow, had the hammer in her left hand, and as she sloshed forward she swapped it with her right.

Klimt reached the bottom of the stairs, slipped, caught himself, and began to scramble up.

Lauren came up behind him. The hammer swung over her head.

"Wait…" Klimt said, raising his hand.

The hammer came down. Once. Twice. The hand fell away. Three times.

Lauren rose up and turned to look at the others. She wore a stern smile. "I've waited too long to do that." She tossed the hammer aside, disappearing in the blood.

Zach looked from Maddie to Colin and back again. Maddie looked surprised, shocked. Colin's expression was unreadable, and then he began to laugh.

"Why are you laughing?" Maddie asked him.

But that only made Colin laugh harder.

Zach smiled, couldn't help himself.

Lauren was laughing too.

Colin could barely speak. "I can't believe this shit," he managed and then rolled over in the blood and howled at the crimson painted wall, at that single accusing eye — all that remained of the mural.

CHAPTER 73
MADDIE

Zach said, still laughing, "You're all here."

Maddie was smiling, chuckling along with the others, but her attention was on the boy who was now standing only a couple feet away, eyes squinted, clutching his side. He'd hugged her and Colin as if he knew them. Where had he come from? He looked familiar, perhaps she'd seen him around the neighborhood, but she could not remember ever speaking with him.

When the laughter had subsided somewhat, she said, "Zach?"

He looked at her.

"What do you know?"

"What? Um…what do you mean?"

The woman who had been with Zach came forward. "Strange kid, huh?" Lauren said. "He saved my life earlier. But I have a nagging suspicion he might actually know what's going on."

Colin looked up, began to rise to his feet; Maddie helped lift him. "Are you okay?" she asked him. "Yeah, I'm good," he said back to her, but his voice was shaky, utterly exhausted.

Lauren stood by Maddie's side. "So tell us, Zach, now that it's over, what's been going on in Mesa Rapids? What was Klimt doing to our town?"

Zach looked at them, his eyes darting from face to face. "Over?" he said. "You still don't underst—"

"Your town?" came a voice from above. "Do you really think this place belongs to you?"

Maddie jumped, she hadn't heard anyone enter the basement. Everyone turned to look up the stairs.

A man stood at the banister, face pale, eyes dark.

"This is my town," the man said. "This has always been my town."

Zach groaned.

"You!" Lauren said. "You're the one who invited me to the—"

"Party?" The man smiled thinly. "Enjoying yourselves?"

"Mr. M. He killed my friend. Oh, god, it's Mr. M," Zach said to himself, holding his head in his hands.

"Who are you?" Maddie asked.

Besides his smile, Mr. M's face was blank. "It's nice to see you again."

Maddie shook her head. "No. I don't think so."

Mr. M laughed, high and piercing.

Zach was crouched at Maddie's feet, rocking and mumbling to himself.

"You," Mr. M said, and Colin flinched, knowing immediately he was being addressed. "Finish what you started."

Colin's neck hinged as he bent back his head to meet Mr. M's gaze with his own. "No," he said quietly. "I won't."

"Yeah," Lauren said. "I think we're done here." Maddie shook her head: no.

Zach stood, shaky but resolute. He opened his mouth: "Go away."

Mr. M's smile did not change; it appeared painted on his gray flesh. "You created me, you and your fathers and mothers—that's why I'm here. It is not my practice to go where I'm not wanted. Finish or die." Something dropped over the banister, splashed, a dark shape floating in the blood. Mr. M faded backward, the shadows folding over him until he was no longer visible.

"Finish it your own damn self," Colin said, but Mr. M was already gone.

They could hear the door close, the latch being drawn.

At least I'm no longer alone, Colin thought.

Slowly, he began to wade across the basement. Maddie followed him, looking worried, that cute scowl line cracking the crusty blood between her eyes. He could hear the others already beginning to look for a way out.

"What is that?" he heard Lauren say, referring to whatever it was Mr. M had dropped.

"His briefcase," Zach said. "Don't open that!"

He heard Zach thrash through the blood and up the stairs. "It's locked," he called down to them. "It's stuck." The sound of his fists pounding and pounding, reverberating through the basement. "Where's that hammer?" Lauren was saying. "Where is that fucking thing?"

When Colin reached the recliner, its seat now hovering above the surface of the blood, he dropped himself, squelching, into it. "Colin? We have to get out of here. Are you okay?"

Colin closed his eyes. "I'm tired…" He could feel himself immediately beginning to drift. "Just a dream…"

"Colin?" It was Maddie's voice, soft and comforting. His eyes fluttered, opening for a minute, and he caught a glimpse of Maddie's shoulder, milky white beneath flaking blood. And the one eye still visible on his mural…

It blinked, slit maliciously.

He jerked awake, his heart pounding.

He could hear Lauren, having joined Zach at the top of the stairs. "Stand back, kid. I grew up on a horse ranch. I know how to use this thing." The sounds of the hammer smashing against the door came down to him. They were trying, but he knew what the others did not: it was no use. "Keep trying," Zach said.

Maybe, he thought, he should just finish covering his fucking mural, paint over that horrible eye, and be done with it.

"Over here," Zach said, now sloshing along the basement floor again. "There's a window. Lauren! Come here!"

And Maddie said, "Is the blood getting deeper?"

Chapter 74
ZACH

Zach heard Maddie's words: "The blood; it's coming from the briefcase."

He climbed nimbly up the piled boxes and various junk to reach the window. It had a latch, but it was stuck, sealed with rust. The glass was greasy and smeared, but he could still see the moon, a fuzzy ball of cream. And it was only glass; they could smash glass. "Lauren," he called out. "Bring your hammer."

"I'm coming. I'm coming."

He heard her sloshing across the basement. Then she was climbing up the junk, a little more carefully than he'd done, but eager to get to the top. She wedged in next to him. "All right, watch your face," she said, and brought the hammer against the glass.

It thumped, but didn't break.

"That was more than enough to break a damn window." Lauren swung the hammer again, with more force: *thump*. She swung again: *thump*.

"I'm gonna get out of the way," Zach said, and began to climb down.

"God damn it," Lauren said, beginning to smash the hammer every which way against the glass without success.

As Zach climbed down he could hear Lauren going to town, angry, but no sound of breaking glass.

He jumped down and sunk into blood up to above his waist.

"It's not gonna work," Colin said from his chair. "If they don't want you to leave, you don't leave. Believe me, I know."

Zach struggled to join the others. Colin was standing now, one arm thrown around Maddie's waist, holding her to him.

"It doesn't matter now," Colin said.

Maddie glanced at Colin. "I've told him not to finish the mural."

Zach looked from one end of the basement to the other, not sure what to do now. "We have to do *something*." The blood was up to his shoulders. Soon he'd be forced to swim again.

"Fuck!" Lauren continued to swing her hammer. "Fuck!"

Zach, now treading in the blood, watched the far wall, in particular a pillar of boxes piled one atop the other all the way to the ceiling. He watched the blood rise, visibly climbing the boxes at an alarming rate.

Finish the mural. Paint the wall with your hands.

Zach kicked himself forward, toward the wall. He was already a better swimmer than he'd been before he'd entered the Upshaw Mansion.

"Where are you going?" Maddie asked him, she and Colin now treading the blood, only their heads above the surface, as if severed and floating.

When Zach reached the wall, the blood buoyed him up to the top of the mural so he could look into that one lone eye. He lifted his hands so he could look at them, dripping blood.

Finish and you will see…

For a moment, the rise of the blood seemed to halt.

He brought his hands to the wall, preparing to smear blood over that single hideous eye, blinding it forever. Out of the corner of his eye, he could see the malignant briefcase bobbing by, its crevasse no longer bleeding like a slit throat.

He blinked.

Zach shook his head. If he finished the mural, something unimaginably horrible was going to happen, something far worse than a little blood. He kicked his foot out, and pushed off from the wall. He swam to join the others—Lauren now with them—huddled together by the window, hanging by the pipes in the ceiling. Maddie smiled at him, and helped him grab one of the pipes.

When he looked back, the blood had covered the eye, nearly all the way to the top.

"Not long now," Colin said.

Chapter 75
THE BIRD

The bird fluttered with a strange sense of purpose. It knew where to go, flitting, bobbing, purring. It knew how to manipulate the cage. The cage was malevolent, wanted to show people things that would hurt them, make them mad. But the bird knew what to do. The bird had an important task to complete, the only task given to it by its creator (whether he'd been aware of it or not), yet it couldn't completely divert the cage from its musings. The cage was doing something, even now, snapping and crunching, blades and drills whirring, splatters dramatic and loud.

Black and vaporous things were emerging from the puddles of blood all around, trying to stop the bird from reaching its destination. They pleaded with the cage, stood in its way, but the bird was in control now and steered the course.

A shadowy limb lashed out and was severed effortlessly by the blades. The cage drove a drill through a bulbous shape, tossed it.

The construct lashed forward and those citizens of Mesa Rapids who saw its flurry of violence turned the other way and ran as fast as they could, and when they reached somewhere safe and out of sight, they laughed and rolled their eyes and tried to breathe. The lucky ones could feel their minds glazing over, going blessedly blank, and welcomed it.

The bird jittered frantically. Its senses were limited, but it knew when it had reached its destination. There was a crash, a great deafening sound, as the canisters of gas were ignited. Light and heat. And the bird knew no more.

The bird was free.

Chapter 76
THE UPSHAW MANSION

The explosion tore open the side of the Upshaw Mansion, the basement window fracturing, the sudden change in pressure forcing out what was in, blood from the opened gash, along with whatever else, spewing forth…

Chapter 76

I remember one time discovering my mother crying over an old letter. I rarely saw her cry—her eyes often filled with sadness, but never to the point of brimming over—and my child's heart immediately went out to her. I ran into her arms.

"Why are you sad, Mom?"

She squeezed me tight. "It's a letter from a woman named Rachel Clemens. She sometimes writes to me."

"Is it bad news?" I asked my mother.

"No, it's not that. It's…"

"Does she live close? Maybe she could come and visit. Maybe that would help."

My mother looked at me through red-rimmed eyes. She tried to smile. She tried to speak, but her words caught in her throat; she choked back a sob.

When she could speak again, she said, "She's dead, honey. She's been dead a long time. She's one of our ancestors. One of our tormented ancestors…"

CHAPTER 77
TOGETHER

They awoke in darkness. They awoke in a dream.

The four companions lifted themselves, sticky. One of them vomited. Together, they crawled through the yard, in the cool air beneath the yellow moon, leaving the Upshaw Mansion behind, pouring them out into the night. When they reached the fence, they dragged themselves to their feet, climbed over, and began to move through the open hills toward the train tracks, where a four-car train that had delivered Mr. Harold Klimt's party supplies for the last time sat parked.

At the front of the house, the party continued to rage; people danced hypnotically, obliviously.

The four companions, now friends instantly and effortlessly bound by a history none of them knew, moved automatically toward the train. The youngest led the way, motivated by an instinct beyond their comprehension but that all of them now trusted. They had to get away from the blood, away from Mesa Rapids. They'd prevented the flood, but Mr. M could still find them if they remained.

They knew who *he* was now.

One of the train cars was open, inviting, as if knowing they were coming, and they helped each other to board. It was filled with wooden crates.

The oldest wanted to leave, but the others stopped her. Despite averted tragedy, Mesa Rapids was no longer safe for them, at least right now. It was best if they left immediately, started their lives anew.

The train began to move. They huddled together. Later, there would be time to talk, although they would find it impossible to describe the true emotional impact of their experience accurately with each other. Words would cheapen what they felt, but they would, nevertheless, try. For now, however, they clutched each other, shivering, crying.

When next the sun rose, Mesa Rapids could lick its wounds, and begin to heal.

PART FIVE

WITHIN

CHAPTER 78

*M*y journal is lost, of course, mired in the basement of the Upshaw
Mansion with the others. Gone. But that's okay. I have a new
one now, although I doubt I'll be writing much for a while.

Maddie has been moody lately; she's pregnant, which makes
it okay, of course. And she still smiles, still seems happy to be
living with me, but sometimes I catch her sighing to herself,
staring sightlessly out a window when she thinks I'm not
looking, as if examining her past, questioning where it went
wrong, and I wonder.

*We like it in Hawthorne, Colorado. It's a small town, small enough
to see the same people every time we go out to the store, but large
enough to have a Starbucks that's always busy, so Maddie and I didn't
have trouble finding employment. We work separate shifts most of the
time, but sometimes they overlap. Sometimes we joke and flirt. I swat
her on the butt with a towel and she giggles and when I'm turned away
pouring espresso, she swats me back. We smile a lot. Our lives are
pretty normal. We're happy, I think, in Hawthorne.*

*You can't find Hawthorne on any of the maps. Even Google Earth
doesn't have it labeled, although I was still able to zoom in and see
the town, even find our rental house, and the train tracks that wind
through the middle of town—the used Honda Accord Maddie's parents
gave us thump-thumping over them every day on the way to work and
on the way back—even though I've never seen any trains pass through.
Still, it was the first town the train brought us to that crazy night we
fled Mesa Rapids and Maddie and I liked it enough to stay. Where else
were we going to go?*

Lauren moved to Denver and we haven't heard much from her. Last we heard she was curating a small art gallery and living with some guy named Eric. You know, like "Eric the Viking," she said in one of her letters. "HaHa." She sent us a copy of her new magazine, *AfterArt*, around the holidays along with a card that said she was doing great and wanted to stay in touch. She said "her man" had asked her to marry him and she'd said no, but that they were still living together. She said she had a lot of tiresome social obligations and then she said something funny. She said she'd gone back to Mesa Rapids, to get her stuff, sell her house, and take care of her father's estate and funeral arrangements. She said Mesa Rapids was getting back to normal; they'd buried their dead and were moving on, but that it somehow no longer felt like home. She said she'd had dreams sometimes about Mesa Rapids, about the things they'd all been through. She said she wanted to talk with us sometime. That it might be important. But it's been months now without contact.

Zach, after lingering in the cramped hotel room in Hawthorne with Maddie and me for several days while we figured out what to do, had to, of course, go back to Mesa Rapids. Being a minor, he had to move back in with his dad, and the authorities had been looking for him and he didn't want to get us in trouble. I offered to drive him back, but he only gave me a sharp look and insisted he'd be fine taking a Greyhound bus. Maddie had him call when he was safely home, and when he finally had, late that same night, he'd said things like: "I'll keep watch" and "Don't worry about me" and "If I see anything strange, I'll let you guys know." He's very mature for his age.

Just the other night, he called and Maddie talked on the phone with him for a long time. He and Maddie are close, especially after Zach was able to find Maddie's dog, Isabel, and have it shipped out to us. After a while, she called me into the kitchen and I took the phone. "Hey, Zach. How're things going out there, man?"

"Hi, Colin. They're good. Haven't seen anything weird. Not yet."

That was a strange thing to say, but I said, "That's good. I'm glad to hear you're doing good. Hey, maybe we can—"

"Listen," Zach said through the phone's receiver. "Maddie won't *tell me, but something's wrong. Do you know what's going on?"*

For some reason, my heart went cold. "I…No. I don't think…"

"Something's still not right."

But then Zach became less serious and we talked about normal things. He told me his dad was doing well in AA, still grouchy, but getting better. He told me he'd made a new friend at school and he'd been hanging out with her a lot after school. "Her? " I asked him, but he was embarrassed and quickly changed the subject. He told me about a dream he'd been having. It seems like every time we talk one of us shares a dream we've had; I guess we have that in common; he reminds me of myself at that age. In the dream, he said, he saw a circle of ancient people, praying over something very large that was buried in the ground. He saw the people had smiles on their faces and they were dancing. Then he saw the people crumble away and realized that what they'd put in the ground was themselves, a mass grave. But then he laughed, silly dreams, right?

He's a smart kid. I hope my own son is half as intelligent as he is.

That's right. It's a boy. Maddie and I are excited. We've been shopping for onesies, cute tiny socks, a crib, everything we're going to need. "We're going to be a family," Maddie says a lot these days. And I smile back and say, "I know." I felt the baby kick the other day and when I looked up at Maddie, amazed, she was smiling, rolled her eyes at me in that cute way, and we made love right there on the couch. It was strange, with her swelling belly between us, but somehow we both knew the baby wanted us to, wanted us to be together and happy. We painted the walls of the extra bedroom a soft green color and Maddie added an elaborate fairy-tale scene, complete with flying sprites, happy gnomes, and benevolently enchanted trees. She wanted me to add my own touch to the walls, but when she tried to hand me the brush, I recoiled.

I haven't painted anything since Mesa Rapids. I've been too scared. I don't want to make the dreams come back. Not now that I've found a way to suppress them.

Not long after Maddie and I settled into our new home in Hawthorne, I began to have horrible nightmares again. I'd awaken in the dark, Maddie furiously shaking me, both of us screaming, me from the nightmare and her from the fear on my contorted face. For a moment, I'd still see the horror of the dream, but then it'd be gone, a trauma too terrible to remember—yet the scars remain.

The dreams became so unbearable, I couldn't sleep. I was plagued every night. I tried to sleep on the couch in the living room, but my screams still woke Maddie, even through the closed bedroom door. We spent long, cold nights together, Maddie trying to comfort me, telling me she was having nightmares too, but her empathy was not helpful. I saw a doctor. We tried sleep therapy, all manner of drugs, including some powerful tranquilizers, but they only made the nightmares worse.

But now my nightmares are finally under control. Maddie helps me because she loves me, because she wants us to have a happy family. She knows what I've been through. She's been through some of it herself. She helps me because she's had horrible dreams too and helping me with what I have to do makes things better for both of us. We're a team.

Still, life is strange. There's always been darkness, lots of empty space to fill.

Just the other day at the grocery store I noticed a woman watching me from the other end of the cereal aisle. She looked familiar. Where had I seen her before? I took a box of Frosted Flakes and tossed it in my cart. She seemed lonely. "Carrie?" I said, looking up, but she was gone.

CHAPTER 79

*I*t *was a good day. Once the screaming stopped, we both felt better.*

CHAPTER 80

I'm afraid I've given the wrong impression. I know my old journal is lost, but if anyone ever finds it, I think he or she may get the wrong idea about my parents, especially my dad. I was loved. I want people to know that. It's just that my dad had a monkey on his back; he was a drunk, and drinking made him angry and irrational. If it wasn't for the alcohol, I'm sure he'd have been an excellent father.

And it wasn't like he didn't try. He wanted to quit drinking, to be a good and loving husband and father. He tried; he really did.

He'd read in a magazine, one he'd happened to pick up from the doctor's office waiting room, of a method used in Eastern medicine to quit drinking that involved intense meditation. In the technique, the afflicted individual was to meditate, clearing the mind of spiritual and emotional toxins, for sixteen hours of the day without speaking. Then one small meal and sleep. Silent the entire time. Then get up the next day and do it again, for seven days, an entire week. During that time, distractions were to be kept at a minimum and the afflicted individual was not allowed to speak or make sounds of any kind.

Having failed all other more traditional methods to quit drinking—therapy, Western medicine, Alcoholics Anonymous, etc.—and with the impending birth of his firstborn, he decided to give the technique a try.

He rented a small apartment away from his wife, empty of distractions and furniture, except for a small rug he placed on the floor by a window overlooking a large cottonwood tree that was to be his only view for seven days. He collected the food and water he would require, took sick leave at work, and made all of the necessary calls and arrangements not to be bothered or worried over for the week. He told

*his wife, now in her final trimester of pregnancy, this was what he had
to do. "For Colin," he said. "It's for little Colin."*

And thus one early November, his period of silence began.

*He watched the wind rock the leaves on the cottonwood tree, its
branches shaking and shivering. He watched birds alighting on those
branches, squabbling, chasing each other: brown finches, and robins,
and once an angry magpie that claimed the tree for nearly an entire
day, striking out at any who tried to enter its territory with its beak.
Some of the leaves began to yellow and fall.*

*It was difficult at first, his concentration ragged, his entire body
shaking with withdrawal. He sweated and he shivered and stank. His
head ached in periodic intervals, pulsing in and out. For a while, he
saw spots.*

*But, after the first couple of days, the physical symptoms withdrew
and he was left feeling only hollow, which was somehow worse. But,
determined to see the week through, he persisted. He was empty, unused
to sobriety and the swirling insecurities that came with it. His mind
told him he was worthless. His mind told him to give up, that there was
a drugstore right around the corner. He was thirsty. He didn't need to
quit drinking altogether, just slow down, keep himself in check.*

*But he knew that wasn't possible; not for him. He had a son coming.
He had to find a new way to fill his emptiness. His son could do that.
He had to be strong for his son, for his beautiful baby boy.*

*And so he remained silent. He remained still, sitting cross-legged
on his prayer rug. He watched the birds, chirping and squawking. He
watched the leaves change color and fall. He watched the tree shiver in
the wind.*

*He tried. He tried so hard. And on his final day, at the very end
of the last hour of the 168 hours of silent meditation, finally, he lifted
himself. Weak but strong, he dressed in his street clothes. It was six a.m.
exactly. He left the apartment.*

*He walked down to the corner drugstore. He stopped at the pay
phone on the outside of the building. He called home and his mother-
in-law told him to call the hospital right away. He called the hospital
and someone put the doctor on the phone, told him he was the father of*

a healthy baby boy, "Here's your wife."

"Stephen? Is that you? " *his wife's breathy voice came to him through the phone's receiver. She sounded exhausted.*

"Yes," *he said.* "It's me. How is he?"

"He's beautiful."

My father was close to tears. "Yeah? "

"Well, actually no. He was purple and covered in goop, but he looks better now that the nurses have cleaned him up a bit." *My father could tell she was smiling.*

My father laughed. He laughed because he felt good. "When was he born? "

"Let me see," *my mother said.* "Looks like twenty-eight minutes ago. At six a.m."

"At sux a.m exactly?"

"That's what the doctor said. Declared it officially. When can you be here?"

"Soon," *my father said, standing perfectly still, eyes unblinking.* "I'll be there very soon."

He tried. He tried very hard.

CHAPTER 81

I have this one dream, one of the ones I remember, where I'm digging through boxes, reading newspaper clippings and old love letters by people long dead, and I discover some kind of rifle under a tangled pile of multicolored paper streamers saved from a party long ago. It is a high-powered weapon, semiautomatic. I don't know what it's called. I don't know a lot about guns.

In the dream, I'm slowly going up the stairs. There's a party going on and I'm the host, neglecting my guests as usual. I make my way down the hall and burst through the double doors. On the other side, there is a large ballroom filled with dancing people. They turn their heads when they see me, smiling and smiling. They applaud. They continue to applaud and smile as I turn the gun down, and depress the trigger.

I awaken then, before I can see the carnage, but, for a minute or two, I can still hear their applause.

And then I know the dreams are coming back, ones far more horrifying than this one, and it's time for another excursion.

It's been easy in Hawthorne. Perhaps because of the train tracks, there are a lot of transients that go through town. We go out at night, invite one over, Maddie and I. We feed him, wrap him in a blanket and warm him by the fire. We offer him whiskey and he always drinks.

When he's good and relaxed, we take him down to the basement. We use knives to release the blood. We let the body hang while the blood drains. We watch the earth hungrily soak up the blood. When that's done, we bury the body in the corner.

Maddie cried the first time and I had to do most of the work, but now she's resigned to it. She says she'd do anything to keep the nightmares away. We even smile now, while we're doing it. Sometimes we flirt, swatting each other's butts with one of the cleaning rags. Once, we made love there in the basement, our bodies still smeared with blood.

The first time, we were nightmare free for six months, but lately it's been more like two or three. That's okay, though. We've never been suspected; nobody cares about the transients; you never see policemen in Hawthorne.

It's a strange place. The other night, at the bar, I even thought I saw Donnie, but it was crowded that night and by the time I got to the door he was already gone.

I love Maddie so much and I know she loves me too. She says so all the time. She's very late in her pregnancy now and we'll have a new member of the family soon.

I'm going to try my hardest. I'm going to be a good father.

Yes, there's emptiness, but always something to fill it. Perhaps one day I'll go back and start painting again.

He is us. He comes from within.

ABOUT THE AUTHOR

"Like Bradbury on acid" (Greg Gifune, *The Bleeding Season*), Keith Deininger is an award-winning author know for blending elements of fantasy with horror in his surreal, literary style. His work is often described as disturbing, surreal and cinematic, "its tutelary spirits are Barker and Lynch, Carpenter and Cronenberg" (Peter Tennant, *Black Static Magazine*) and he has been called "one of the finest writers of imaginative fiction out there" (Craig Saunders, *Deadlift*).

Deininger grew up in Colorado Springs, Colorado where he wrote some of his first stories while in grade school, odd tales about finding dead people in the basement and about waking up in strange worlds. He then moved to Los Alamos, New Mexico where, in high school, he won first place in a science fiction writing contest judged by Ray Bradbury, who presented him with the award and said, "I really enjoyed your story."

In college, at the University of New Mexico where he received his BA in creative writing, Deininger focused for a time on poetry, winning an Editor's Choice Award in the literary magazine *Conceptions Southwest* for his poem "Grandma."

His first novel, *The New Flesh*, was published in 2013 to critical acclaim, called a "dark and sinister debut" (Ronald Malfi, *Little Girls*), and Deininger hailed as a "prodigious talent" (Jon Bassoff, *Corrosion*). His follow up, Ghosts of Eden, was equally well received as a "twisted masterpiece" (Allan Leverone, Tracie Tanner thrillers) and a "psychedelic journey through alternative realities, familial relationships and the mysteries of the mind." Deininger has since published several novels and novellas, including the horror novel *Within* ("Best horror 2015",

Michael Patrick Hicks) and the "Mcarthyesque fever-dream" (C. M. Muller) *Fevered Hills*. He is also the author of *A Game for Gods*, the first title in a highly anticipated, literary and imaginative dark fantasy series.

You can find more information on the author and his work on:

Twitter: @keithdeininger
Facebook: keith.deininger
Goodreads: keithdeininger
Or visit his official website www.KeithDeininger.com

Curious about other Crossroad Press books?
Stop by our site:
http://store.crossroadpress.com
We offer quality writing
in digital, audio, and print formats.

Enter the code FIRSTBOOK
to get 20% off your first order from our store!
Stop by today!